# A Blessing for the Reader

*"May the words you read here remind you that God sees, God heals, and God redeems every trial. May you find courage to walk through your own fire with hope and faith."*

May these pages become more than just a story to you. May they be a mirror where you recognize your own scars and a window through which you see God's faithfulness. As you walk through each chapter, may you hear the whisper of the Spirit saying, *"You are not alone."*

If you carry wounds that no one else has seen, may these words remind you that the God who brought me through will also carry you. If you feel forgotten, may you encounter the One who never forgets His children. And if you feel weary from the flames, may you find strength in knowing that God has a purpose in the fire and a promise beyond the smoke.

# Dedication

*To the broken, the silenced, and the unseen—*

May you know that God sees, God hears, and God delivers.

This book is for every heart that has been betrayed, every voice that has been muted, and every soul that has ever wondered if God still cares. You are not forgotten. Your tears are not wasted. Your prayers are not unheard.

*"The Lord is close to the brokenhearted and saves those who are crushed in spirit."*

— Psalm 34:18

May this testimony be a reminder that no matter how fierce the fire, God is faithful to bring you through.

# LIVING IN GEHENNA

## Faith in the Midst of Fire

**Dr. Cordell Brown.**

*"When you walk through the fire, you will not be burned; the flames will not set you ablaze."*

— Isaiah 43:2

Dr. Cordell Brown-FRONTLINE PUBLISHING

EBook ISBN: 979-8-89795-905-1

Paperback: 979-8-89795-963-1

Hardcover:  979-8-89795-964-8

First Edition

Printed in the United States of America

# Table of Contents

# Preface

This is a true story. The details are real, the wounds were deep, and the journey—though painful—was never without purpose.

Like the Joseph of the Bible, I endured betrayal by someone close, manipulation masked as affection, and a season of deep emotional and spiritual imprisonment. Yet also like him, I found that God was with me in every step—from the pit to the prison, and ultimately, toward healing.

*"But the Lord was with Joseph and extended kindness to him…"* (Genesis 39:21)

The woman to whom I was married will be referred to as **Zuleika**, a name traditionally given to Potiphar's wife—the woman who falsely accused Joseph and attempted to control him through deceit and desire. This choice is not made in malice, but to symbolize the nature of what took place in my story: the misuse of intimacy, manipulation under the guise of love, and the distortion of covenant.

This book is not written in anger. It is not a weapon. It is a testimony.

It exists to give voice to what so many suffer in silence. It is for the man or woman walking through their own Gehenna, believing no one would understand. It is for those whose spiritual and emotional abuse was hidden beneath religious language, behind closed doors, or beneath the surface of what seemed like a godly life.

*"Nothing is hidden that will not be made manifest, nor is anything secret that will not be known and come to light."* (Luke 8:17)

You are not alone.

This story is mine, but its message is for anyone who has endured manipulation, emotional bondage, or spiritual confusion in the name of love. You may see your story in mine. My prayer is that these words—rooted in Scripture and poured out through pain—will help you see that even in the furnace, God walks with you.

*"You intended to harm me, but God intended it for good, to accomplish what is now being done, the saving of many lives."* (Genesis 50:20)

This Preface is my invitation to you: walk with me through the pages ahead, not as a spectator but as a fellow traveler. Whether your fire was lit by betrayal, injustice, or spiritual oppression, know that God is the same yesterday, today, and forever. The same God who carried Joseph through his prison and raised him into purpose is the same God who still delivers today.

This book is not only my testimony—it is a mirror for anyone who has been silenced, doubted, or wounded. It is also a window, opening onto the greater story of God's faithfulness. If you find yourself in the furnace, take courage: the fire will not consume you. Instead, it will refine you, just as it has refined me.

# Author's Note / Content Warning

The content of this book includes references to emotional, spiritual, and psychological abuse within the context of a marriage. While no explicit details are given, readers who have experienced similar trauma may find certain chapters triggering. I encourage you to read prayerfully and take breaks as needed.

If at any point you feel overwhelmed, I urge you to pause and remind yourself:

- You are not weak for feeling.
- You are not alone in your pain.
- And you are not without hope.

God is still a healer, and His Word remains your anchor.

*"The Lord is close to the brokenhearted and saves those who are crushed in spirit."* (Psalm 34:18)

I also encourage you to invite trusted support into your journey as you read. Whether that is a counselor, a pastor, or a close friend, do not carry the weight of these pages in isolation. Healing often happens in community, and while my story may mirror your pain, God has also placed people in your life who can walk with you toward wholeness.

Above all, let this note serve as a reminder: you are not reading this book as a victim, but as a survivor in the making. Every page is written with the prayer that the God who met me in my fire will meet you in yours.

# Introduction

Every life tells a story. Some are filled with celebration and peace; others are marked by heartbreak and loss. Most—like mine—hold both. Mine is a story carved by suffering but anchored in redemption. It is not just a testimony of survival, but a declaration of the faithfulness of God in the midst of devastation.

For years, I lived in what felt like Gehenna—a personal hell defined by torment, deception, and deep oppression. It wasn't just emotional; it was spiritual and physical. The very places that should have been sacred became unsafe. The people who should have been protected became the ones who were wounded. What should have been a covenant of love turned into a crucible of pain. I wore a smile on the outside, but inside, I was crumbling.

But God—two of the most powerful words in all of Scripture.

*"But God demonstrates His own love for us in this: While we were still sinners, Christ died for us."* (Romans 5:8)

Even in the fire, even in the lies, even in the silence, God was present. Not as a distant observer, but as an ever-present help in trouble (Psalm 46:1). His nearness did not always remove the pain, but it gave me strength to endure it. His voice did not always silence the accusers, but it reminded me of my true identity when theirs sought to strip it away.

When I felt forgotten, I remembered:

*"Can a mother forget the baby at her breast and have no compassion on the child she has borne? Though she may forget, I will not forget you."* (Isaiah 49:15)

When I felt voiceless, I held to:

*"The righteous cry out, and the Lord hears them; He delivers them from all their troubles."* (Psalm 34:17)

When I questioned my worth, I clung to:

*"You are precious and honored in my sight, and... I love you."* (Isaiah 43:4)

This book is not just about the realities of abuse, manipulation, or suffering—it is about what God can do in the middle of it. It is about how the Word of God becomes breath to the breathless, hope to the hopeless, and strength to the weary. It is about the process of healing, the discipline of trusting, and the beauty of rediscovery.

And yes, I want people to learn from what I endured.

I want you to recognize the early signs of spiritual and emotional manipulation—when someone uses Scripture to control rather than to set free, when fear is disguised as faith, when silence is forced rather than chosen.

I want you to understand that abuse can wear a thousand disguises, and sometimes it looks like righteousness, but its fruit is always rotten.

*"By their fruit you will recognize them."* (Matthew 7:16)

I want you to know that being a Christian doesn't mean submitting to suffering that God never asked you to endure.

*"It is for freedom that Christ has set us free."* (Galatians 5:1)

The chapters ahead will walk you through my valley—the slow, creeping erosion of self-worth, the lies I believed, the compromises I made, and the moments when I almost gave up. But they will also show you how the Lord gently rebuilt what was broken.

*"He heals the brokenhearted and binds up their wounds."* (Psalm 147:3)

If you are reading this and you are still in your Gehenna, I want you to know:

- You are not weak because you're hurting.
- You are not faithless because you're afraid.
- And you are not alone.

*"Even though I walk through the valley of the shadow of death, I will fear no evil, for You are with me."* (Psalm 23:4)

This is my story. This is my offering. Not just to tell the truth, but to teach through it. My prayer is that my pain would become your wisdom—and that my healing would point you toward yours.

Let this be your reminder:

*"When you pass through the waters, I will be with you; and when you pass through the rivers, they will not sweep over you. When you walk through the fire, you will not be burned."* (Isaiah 43:2)

God doesn't waste pain. He redeems it.

This is my testimony.

This is my declaration:

*"I can do all things through Christ who strengthens me."* (Philippians 4:13)

And this is my invitation: walk with me through these pages, not as a detached reader, but as one who may see reflections of your own journey in mine. If you are in the fire, know that God is with you. If you have come through, may this story affirm that He wastes nothing. Either way, may you finish these pages not only with understanding, but with renewed faith, knowing that every fire has its end—and every end in Christ carries the seed of a new beginning.

# Chapter 1 – The Beginning of the Fire

*"Hope deferred maketh the heart sick: but when the desire cometh, it is a tree of life." (Proverbs 13:12)*

Hope is a powerful thing. It doesn't just light the dark—it distorts it. It blurs the cracks in the walls you should see clearly, dulls the sharp edge of warnings meant to protect you, and whispers that love can mend what only truth has the strength to reveal. My story begins, as so many do, in hope. But it was not the soft hope of comfort or privilege. Mine was a harder kind, forged in the fire of hardship—tempered by loss, sharpened by struggle, and carried like a shield into a world that offered no promises..

## Childhood and the Forge of Resilience

I grew up in poverty, in a home where hunger was more than an occasional visitor—it was a familiar companion at the table. Nights stretched long and cold, endured beneath thin blankets that did little to stop the chill seeping through the drafty house. The wooden floorboards groaned beneath my small, bare feet, and the wind whistled through cracks in the windows like an uninvited guest.

Sometimes, when the air was sharpest, the faint smell of wood smoke from our neighbor's stove would drift in, a reminder of warmth we did not have.

My childhood was a landscape of missed opportunities and dreams put on hold, painted in shades of scarcity. Yet even there, amid lack and longing, I stumbled upon an unlikely refuge—books. Their pages offered more than stories; they offered escape, possibility, and the quiet promise that there was a world beyond mine. Education became my sanctuary, a doorway into places untouched by poverty, where hope was not a fantasy but a seed waiting to be nurtured.

I excelled academically, driven by the belief that if I could just be good enough, if I could prove my worth through success, the world would see me—not as the poor, neglected child—but as someone of value. I spent countless hours at the library to complete assignments, often scribbling notes under the dim glow of a flickering lamp.

When there were no textbooks, I read books on display at bookstores to finish assignments. There was no money to photocopy pages, so I wrote everything down by hand, making the most of every opportunity to learn.

Even in hardship, God's presence was quietly shaping me. My grandmother, the woman who raised me, often prayed over me at night. She would whisper Scriptures into my ears, reminding me that God sees the heart, not the outward condition. I remember sitting by her bedside as she held my small hands, telling me, "God has a plan for you, even when the world doesn't see it."

My uncles used to joke about the size of my head; they laughed and called me names. Grandma, however, would always steady us with a grin and a quiet confidence: "Child, your head's the way it is because you've got a brain in it. One day you'll wrap those boys up with your knowledge." Her words felt like a small, stubborn shield.

Those moments, though small, planted seeds of faith that would later grow strong in the furnace of trials.

It was in those whispered Scriptures that I first learned what it meant to have a destiny beyond circumstances. My grandmother could not give me wealth, but she gave me something richer: the conviction that God Himself was invested in my story. That seed would keep me through the darkest seasons of life.

Yet, poverty has a way of leaving scars, even when hidden. At my middle school graduation, a teacher publicly gave me a gift for being the "Most Needy Student." It stung deeply. Though I had excelled in national exams, her words reduced me to nothing more than my economic condition. That moment stayed with me, carving a wound I buried but never truly healed. It planted a seed of a lie: that no matter how much I achieved, I would still be seen as "less than."

"The tongue has the power of life and death" (Proverbs 18:21). Those words became more real over time, because what started as one teacher's misjudgment would later echo in whispers of control and criticism within my marriage.

During my second year of high school, the trauma of losing my grandmother hit me like a tidal wave. She became ill and passed away, and with her death, I lost a source of stability and love. My performance slipped. I lost interest in everything I once cared about. The grief was suffocating. I could still hear her voice in my dreams, urging me to trust God even when I could not understand why life was so hard. Nights were long, filled with quiet sobs and prayers whispered in the dark. My pillow would be soaked, and I would clutch my Bible for comfort, reading passages over and over until I could feel my breathing slow. But the seeds of faith she had planted held firm. Upon the death of my grandmother, I stole hard liquor from the wake, would take it to school, and drink to numb the pain.

By my third year, challenges compounded. My history teacher imposed his atheist convictions on the class, attempting to sway us from our beliefs. With the guidance of my pastor, I chose to hold firm to my faith, even when it put me at odds with authority. That same year, my chemistry teacher displayed blatant favoritism, giving private lab lessons to select students and failing the rest. When confronted years later about crushing my dream of becoming a medical doctor, he remained unapologetic, cementing the anger I felt at his racism and injustice.

The bitterness of that disappointment burned, but so did the resolve it birthed. If doors closed unfairly, I would search for the windows God opened. If people denied me an opportunity, I would trust God to redeem the years. These fires, though cruel, were molding me to rely less on human approval and more on divine calling.

Even then, I began to notice a pattern in my life: moments of injustice, disappointment, and betrayal often coincided with the growth of character traits I would rely on later—resilience, discernment, and patience. I did not always recognize it at the time, but the "little fires" of my youth were shaping a heart that would endure far greater flames. I began to understand that God sometimes allows trials not to punish us, but to prepare us.

The struggle deepened after my baptism in my first year of high school. Another community member, related to the first and also tied to the occult, scoffed that I would not last long in church. With cruel certainty, she said I was destined to be like my womanizing father. But the devil is a liar. Over thirty years later, those words never took root and never came to pass. God's Word, not curses, defines my destiny.

But opposition was not only found in classrooms. It came from the community itself, often cloaked in darkness. As I prepared to enter high school, a community member—well known to be involved in the occult—tried offering me school supplies. My parents, discerning the evil intent, rejected the offer immediately. It was a reminder that not every gift is a blessing; some are snares.

Yet rejection did not only come from the world—it came from within the **church**, the place that should have been my refuge. Around age fourteen, my Sunday school teacher heard a rumor that I had a girlfriend (a false claim, since I wasn't even speaking to that person). Instead of asking me, she called me a derogatory name, "village ram," in front of others. Another time, after walking a church sister to the bus stop, another member accused us of being romantically involved and demanded we "break it off." Innocence was stained with suspicion, and trust was replaced with humiliation.

But the abuse from within the church deepened as I grew older. After graduating high school, I proudly wore my graduation ring—a simple token of accomplishment. Yet the youth leader, known for her "holier-than-thou" spirit, was offended by it. She refused to fellowship with me. One Sunday morning, while the choir was singing and I was playing the organ, she was leading the choir. In her bitterness, she stopped directing and walked away, refusing to lead as long as I was present. Decades later, she has not changed, still operating in the same spirit of division.

These early attacks planted confusion: why would the very people entrusted with my spiritual care choose judgment over guidance? Why would the house of God feel as hostile as the world outside?

## Fire Before the Fire: Senior Year

By the time I reached 12th grade, something shifted for the worse. After hours spent in the library completing an assignment, a classmate asked to see it. I willingly obliged. He copied it and turned it in as his own, earning 11/12, while I was given 4/12.

The instructor coldly accused me of being incapable of producing such work. I only received credit because it was a calculation she couldn't dispute. To make matters worse, she was involved with the married vice principal. When their relationship soured, I was given an ultimatum: leave the school, or she would. The administration sided with her. Pleas, interventions, and appeals all failed. My education, my dignity, and my future were cast aside because of corruption and immorality in high places. Another reason they wanted me out was because I was next in line to be the Head Boy and they wanted to put a politician's son in that position.

"How long will you defend the unjust and show partiality to the wicked?" (Psalm 82:2)

These wounds cut deep because they came not from strangers but from those I worshipped beside. They revealed how jealousy, bitterness, and legalism can masquerade as holiness — and how dangerous church hurt can be when left unchecked.

Even in these moments, small glimpses of God's faithfulness were present. A teacher who genuinely cared, a friend who encouraged me, and the Scriptures I clung to became lifelines. These early experiences of betrayal and injustice foreshadowed future trials in relationships and spiritual warfare, teaching me that endurance and discernment are as important as knowledge or achievement. I began to sense that life would test not only my mind but my spirit.

## College-Level Struggles and Spiritual Warfare

Unable to afford university tuition, I enrolled in college-level continuing education courses. Again, I excelled. One paper earned a 98%, and my instructor remarked that it was as if I had read his mind. But excellence attracts envy. A fellow student, irritated by my success, muttered that I was "too smart for my own good."

Soon, I faced an unimaginable trial: the powers of darkness rose against me. Witchcraft and spiritual attacks left me severely ill, tormented nightly by demons. I became a shell of myself, losing significant weight and developing intense fear. At 20, I returned to my parents' room to sleep, terrified of being alone.

Yet the church, family, and community did not stop praying. Deliverance came, not overnight, but steadily, through the power of Jesus Christ. I remember sitting in my room, trembling, yet sensing the presence of God gradually restoring peace to my spirit. Every small victory felt monumental: a night without terror, a meal eaten in peace, a fear that slowly lifted.

But even as God gave me victories, new forms of opposition appeared. When I completed college and wrote a book—donating every penny of the proceeds to charity—I expected encouragement. The book launch was held during one of our youth convocations. People were excited, inspired, and hopeful. Yet in the midst of the celebration, one of the bishops—consumed by anger—took the microphone. In front of the congregation, he mocked my credentials, declaring, *"I don't care about the letters you have behind your name. You could have D-O-G S-H-I-T and you don't have Jesus!"*

I was humiliated. Not because his words were true, but because they were spoken publicly by a leader. The same community that should have affirmed faith and diligence instead chose to tear down. But I held fast to the truth: I was truly saved, covered by the blood of Jesus, and no insult could undo that reality.

I completed an associate degree while waiting for my student loan and then advanced to a four-year college, ultimately earning a bachelor's degree. With the support of family, friends, and church, I completed two master's degrees and two doctorate degrees.

"What man meant for evil, God turned for good" (Genesis 50:20)

Every fiery trial of my youth forged a faith that would carry me through greater fires yet to come.

# Entering Marriage with Hope

I did not step into life expecting torment—I stepped in believing in love, covenant, and the promises of God I had been taught to trust. From a young age, I carried the belief that marriage was not just a union, but a sacred calling. I imagined it as a partnership built on trust and devotion, a reflection of Christ's love for the Church—selfless, sacrificial, and enduring. I believed in the beauty of two lives becoming one, bound together not only by vows but by faith.

When I said yes to love, I said yes with my whole heart. I believed that prayer could cover wounds before they formed, that forgiveness would always be stronger than failure, and that if we kept God at the center, no storm could truly break us. I entered marriage with hope, not fear—with a faith so strong that I thought it could carry both of us, even when the weight grew heavy.

"Husbands, love your wives, just as Christ loved the church and gave Himself up for her." (Ephesians 5:25)

In the beginning, everything seemed affirming: prayers together, ministry service, Scripture discussions, and shared dreams. "Two are better than one… If either of them falls, the one will lift up his companion." (Ecclesiastes 4:9–10)

But cracks formed silently. Sharp tones, dismissive glances, and controlling suggestions disguised as care began to erode my confidence. I clung to 1 Corinthians 13:4–5, believing patience and endurance were marks of holiness.

Yet subtle control grew into a furnace. Independence faded. Confidence chipped away. Words became weapons. "The tongue has the power of life and death" (Proverbs 18:21)

Like Samson, I had trusted too easily. "Then she called, 'Samson, the Philistines are upon you!' He awoke from his sleep… but he did not know that the Lord had left him." (Judges 16:20)

I pressed on, believing suffering in silence was spiritual, only to realize not every burden is from God. Some are planted by the enemy.

"Catch for us the foxes, the little foxes that ruin the vineyards." (Song of Solomon 2:15)

Even in the fire, God's presence remained:

"The Lord will rescue me from every evil attack and will bring me safely to His heavenly kingdom." (2 Timothy 4:18)

"When you walk through the fire, you will not be burned; the flames will not set you ablaze." (Isaiah 43:2)

The beginning of the fire was not the end—it was the beginning of deliverance. What looked like destruction became the very place where God began to rebuild me. In the heat of every trial, when the flames licked at the edges of my faith, He was there—steady, unshaken, and near. The fire that threatened to consume me became the furnace where He refined me, burning away what was broken, what was false, what was never meant to remain.

God met me there, flame by flame. He walked with me through the smoke of confusion, through the ashes of loss, through the nights when I thought the fire would take everything I had left. Yet each ember carried His presence, each spark whispered His promise: *you will not be destroyed—you will be delivered.* What the enemy meant to break me, God used to make me new.

## Transition to Chapter 2: Meeting Zuleika

As I stepped into the next phase of life, armed with hard-earned resilience, faith, and hope, I believed that love would mirror the promises of God I had clung to through every trial. It was during this season that I met Zuleika, a presence that brought excitement, warmth, and the hope of partnership I had longed for. At first, everything seemed aligned with God's plan—prayers whispered together, shared dreams, and the promise of companionship. Yet beneath the surface, subtle challenges waited, ones I could not yet perceive.

In her, I glimpsed the possibility of covenant and joy, unaware that the lessons of discernment, patience, and steadfast faith I had carried since childhood would soon be tested in ways far beyond anything I had imagined.

This meeting marked the beginning of a chapter filled with both hope and fire—a fire that would shape, challenge, and ultimately refine every part of who I was. I would soon learn that not all trials come from circumstance; some come through people we trust, and through them, God would teach me lessons no book or classroom ever could.

# Chapter 2 – The Mask of Righteousness

**"Satan himself masquerades as an angel of light."**

**(2 Corinthians 11:14)**

## The Subtle Entrance

The beginning of the fire was not the end—it was the beginning of deliverance. What looked like destruction became the very place where God began to rebuild me. In the heat of every trial, when the flames licked at the edges of my faith, He was there—steady, unshaken, and near. The fire that threatened to consume me became the furnace where He refined me, burning away what was broken, what was false, what was never meant to remain.

God met me there, flame by flame. He walked with me through the smoke of confusion, through the ashes of loss, through the nights when I thought the fire would take everything I had left. Yet each ember carried His presence, each spark whispered His promise: *you will not be destroyed—you will be delivered.* What the enemy meant to break me, God used to make me new.

## Meeting Zuleika

I first encountered Zuleika when I began attending that church. My aunt was already a devoted member, and since I lived with her at the time, it felt natural—almost expected—that I would join her there. The congregation was warm and welcoming, filled with familiar rhythms of worship and fellowship, but even in that crowded room, Zuleika stood out.

It wasn't her beauty that first caught my attention, but her presence. She was loud, brash, and determined to be noticed, as if the sanctuary itself couldn't contain her energy. While others seemed charmed by her boldness—perhaps even drawn to it—I felt something different. To me, it came across as disruptive, a kind of performance that demanded more attention than reverence. My first impression was not admiration but irritation. She wasn't my type, and I felt no spark of interest—only the certainty that our paths, though crossing in the same church, had little reason to intertwine.

Yet she made no secret of her pursuit. Dressed sharply, strutting past me with a model's flair, tossing glances and flirtatious remarks, she worked tirelessly to capture my attention. I kept my conversations with her minimal, careful not to encourage what I saw as immaturity. Still, she was relentless, and though I resisted, she seemed to orbit my life with an insistence I couldn't ignore.

Proverbs warns:

"With persuasive words she led him astray; she seduced him with her smooth talk. All at once he followed her like an ox going to the slaughter." (Proverbs 7:21–22)

At the time, I didn't see myself in those verses. I believed my guard was strong. Yet little by little, cracks were forming.

## Was I Under a Spell?

The dating began only after she returned from her trip, and looking back, I know the timing was no coincidence. Before she left, I could hardly tolerate her presence. Her mannerisms grated on me, her personality felt overbearing, and I was convinced she was the last person I would ever be drawn to. But when she came back, something was different—though it wasn't anything outward that had changed. It was me.

It was as though a switch had been flipped inside me. Suddenly, the same voice that once irritated me now caught my attention. The same presence that had felt disruptive now seemed magnetic. I found myself leaning in instead of turning away, curious instead of closed off. The shift was abrupt, undeniable, and impossible to explain by natural means. What I had once dismissed, I was now drawn toward, as if an unseen hand had turned my heart in her direction.

Her father's background—a man rumored to be involved in witchcraft and spiritual practices—made me wonder whether some form of spiritual influence had been at play. It was as though the connection between us wasn't entirely natural, but something deeper, something almost otherworldly. I wasn't just falling in love with her; it felt like I was being pulled into something I couldn't fully understand.

Could it have been that I was under some form of spiritual manipulation? Maybe. Spiritual forces are real, and the Bible speaks of the very real presence of deception that comes through spiritual means:

"For we wrestle not against flesh and blood, but against principalities, against powers, against the rulers of the darkness of this world, against spiritual wickedness in high places." (Ephesians 6:12)

Was I under a spell? Perhaps the term is not too far off.

## The Park Bench

Still, there were moments that felt genuine. I remember sitting with Zuleika on a park bench, the air cool, the sound of children playing in the distance, and the faint golden glow of the evening sun settling around us. She laughed often—too loudly, perhaps—but there was something disarming about her presence.

As we sat and talked, I felt something stirring—a pull that began to loosen the grip of my loneliness and replace it with a fragile, dangerous hope. For so long, I had been searching for love, craving the comfort of companionship, and there she was—eager, available, and undeniably persistent in her pursuit of me. My heart began to soften, not because Zuleika had changed, but because I wanted to believe she could be the answer to my longing.

In that moment, I convinced myself that perhaps this was God's provision, the fulfillment of promises I had prayed over and waited for. I mistook her persistence for purpose, her availability for destiny. What I didn't realize then was that sometimes the heart, in its hunger, will dress up desire as divine will. And so I leaned in, not because I was certain, but because I was desperate to believe.

James warns:

"Each person is tempted when they are dragged away by their own evil desire and enticed. Then, after desire has conceived, it gives birth to sin…" (James 1:14-15)

I did not sin with her. I guarded my integrity fiercely. Yet desire, even restrained, can make the heart susceptible.

## Boundaries and Illusions

I recall one day visiting Zuleika at her apartment. She appeared provocatively attired, and I rebuked her sharply, urging her to cover herself. To my surprise, instead of taking offense, she later confessed to a senior member of our church that I was a true man of God because I had spoken up. For all her forwardness, she seemed to respect my boundaries in that regard, as though my firmness gave her a line she had not been willing—or perhaps able—to draw for herself.

Yet even as she displayed restraint in some areas, there were inconsistencies that unsettled me. Zuleika often wore a cloak of self-righteousness, presenting herself as deeply spiritual, but when pressed, her knowledge of Scripture was shallow at best. Her faith seemed more performance than practice, more about appearances than transformation. She loved to greet people loudly with phrases like, *"Hi, Jesus loves you!"*—a declaration meant to inspire, yet it rang rehearsed, more like a script than a conviction.

But what concerned me most was her evasiveness. When conversations turned serious—about finances, her job, her past, or her family background—she became vague, dismissive, and visibly uncomfortable, as though the truth was something to be concealed rather than shared. These contradictions gnawed at me. They whispered that something wasn't adding up, that the person she wanted others to see was not the whole of who she really was.

Still, I silenced those warnings. I pushed them aside with the hope that patience would eventually yield clarity, that love would bridge the gaps I could not explain. I convinced myself that faith could smooth over the rough edges and that God's grace, working through me, would be enough to redeem what felt lacking in her. What I did not yet understand was that denial, dressed as hope, can be one of the most dangerous lies we tell ourselves.

## The Mask of Righteousness

At first, the signs of deception were imperceptible. How could I have known? Zuleika was so good at creating the illusion of righteousness. She wore the mask of a devoted Christian, deeply involved in church activities, presenting herself as someone who worked hard for the family and spoke often of faith.

The subtlety of her deception was its power; it didn't feel like a lie, but rather like a shadow of truth. She would sprinkle her speech with Scripture, framing her actions in a way that appeared noble.

*"Those who work their land will have abundant food, but those who chase fantasies have no sense."* (Proverbs 12:11)

Yet behind that veneer of diligence was a life that did not align with her claims.

The first time I stopped by her apartment in the morning, everything seemed fine. She was getting ready, as she claimed, to leave for work. There was nothing overtly suspicious—until I decided to stay outside one day, hiding in the parking lot, waiting to see if she would actually leave. But she never did.

The mask of righteousness cracked. Zuleika wasn't working. She was home, hiding behind carefully crafted illusions.

**Reflection Moment:** How often do we accept appearances at face value, especially when they are cloaked in faith language? Are there shadows behind the light you are trusting?

## A Kingdom of Lies

Zuleika's lies weren't isolated slips of the tongue—they were threads in a much larger web she had carefully spun around herself. At first, they seemed harmless, small inconsistencies that I brushed off as misunderstandings. But over time, a pattern emerged. I began to see how deliberately she wove her words, how each half-truth and vague explanation fit into a framework designed to protect her image and keep others—especially me—from looking too closely.

Her use of spiritual language was one of her most powerful tools. Phrases like *"I'm doing this for the Lord,"* or, *"God understands"* seemed righteous on the surface, but in reality, they were shields, crafted to deflect scrutiny. Whenever I pressed her on something that didn't add up—finances, commitments, or past experiences— she cloaked her evasions in holy words. And because I valued faith, I was hesitant to challenge what was wrapped in the language of devotion.

It took me time to realize that these words weren't flowing from a heart surrendered to God—they were a means of control, a way to manipulate trust and silence questions. What I had mistaken for spiritual sincerity was, in truth, spiritual theater, performed with just enough conviction to keep me second-guessing my own discernment. And the more I ignored the small alarms in my spirit, the more entangled I became in her carefully constructed world.

"There is a way that appears to be right, but in the end, it leads to death." (Proverbs 14:12)

Each time I accepted her explanations, I unknowingly stepped further into the fog of manipulation.

**Reflection Moment:** Consider how spiritual language could be used to manipulate in your life. Are there phrases or teachings that demand obedience without love?

## The Tension of Manipulation and Faith

I told myself that dating and preparing for marriage meant sacrifice, that I was just enduring for the sake of peace. But in truth, my patience was becoming a breeding ground for manipulation. I had confused suffering with sacrifice, endurance with submission.

"Let us fix our eyes on Jesus, the author and perfecter of our faith, who for the joy set before Him endured the cross…" (Hebrews 12:2)

Christ's endurance led to victory. Mine was leading me into bondage.

"My people are destroyed for lack of knowledge…" (Hosea 4:6)

## The Consequences of Deception: A House of Lies

The closer we moved toward marriage, the more I realized I was not building a sanctuary of love and faith, but slowly walking into a prison of confusion and control. What should have been a season filled with joy, clarity, and mutual growth was marked instead by unease. The warmth that ought to accompany genuine love was absent, replaced by a creeping chill I could not ignore.

Her vague answers and evasive behavior became recurring patterns—shadows that followed us everywhere. When pressed about important matters—her job, her finances, her past—her responses were consistently blurred, as if truth was always just beyond my grasp. And whenever my spirit stirred with questions, she was quick to cloak her actions in religious language, phrases like *"God understands,"* or *"I'm doing this for the Lord."* At first, they sounded pious, even comforting. But over time, I began to sense how those words were being used, not to point us toward God, but to silence me.

This, I came to understand, was the very heart of spiritual manipulation. It is not loud or obvious—it is subtle, deliberate, and deeply corrosive. It works by sowing doubt, twisting truth just enough that you begin to question your own perception, your own discernment. It blurs the line between faith and fear, until you're no longer sure if you're following God's will or simply being controlled by someone else's voice. The tragedy of it lies in its disguise: it borrows the language of faith but drains it of sincerity, using holy words as chains rather than as freedom.

What unsettled me most was how easily I excused these things at the time. I told myself patience was godliness, that love would eventually smooth over the cracks. But manipulation thrives in the space where discernment is silenced and red flags are rebranded as tests of faith. Instead of peace, I found myself living in a constant tension—drawn in by the hope of covenant, yet quietly aware that I was binding myself to something far from holy.

"The Lord detests lying lips, but He delights in people who are trustworthy." (Proverbs 12:22)

## Prayer Starters for Chapter 2

- Lord, help me discern deception when it masquerades as righteousness.
- Father, give me clarity in relationships cloaked in religious language.
- Jesus, guide me to distinguish godly endurance from harmful passivity.
- Holy Spirit, protect my heart from spiritual manipulation and lies.

## Reflection Questions for Chapter 2

- How can spiritual language be used to manipulate, even unintentionally?
- Are there people in your life whose words and actions don't align? How do you navigate this?
- How do you discern godly patience versus endurance that harms your spirit?
- What steps can you take to align your perceptions with God's truth?

## Transition to Chapter 3

By the time we were planning our wedding, I thought I was stepping into a future filled with joy. In truth, I was walking into a furnace I could not yet see. What began as excitement and hope would soon turn into a daily reality of fire. The very covenant I longed for became the crucible where God would test, refine, and ultimately deliver me.

# Chapter 3 – The Silent Surrender

"Hope deferred makes the heart sick." (Proverbs 13:12)

— Losing your voice while trying to preserve peace.

## A Bridge Between Hope and Heartache

Despite the red flags, despite the unease that gnawed at my spirit, I pressed forward. Hope blinded me, convincing me that marriage would fix what dating had already revealed. I mistook silence for peace and ignored the whispers of wisdom that told me to wait like so many others who long for love. I convinced myself that things would get better once the covenant was made.

Then came the wedding—the day that was supposed to mark the beginning of joy, but instead became the stage for heartbreak.

## The Wedding That Wasn't

The week leading up to the wedding, I felt the weight of doubt pressing hard on my heart. I even picked up the phone and called Mother Merle—the trusted mother of the church I respected deeply. I confessed my second thoughts about the wedding, hoping she might confirm what my spirit already felt. But instead, she encouraged me to press on. Her words were steady and assuring, and because I trusted her so deeply, I leaned into her counsel instead of my unease.

But as the days ticked closer, Zuleika's behavior worsened. She constantly changed her mind about food items for the reception and about decorations, even in the final days leading up to the wedding. My Aunt Peaches, along with some of her friends, had stepped in unofficially to help with some of the food preparations, and every last-minute adjustment from Zuleika sent them into a frenzy. The maid of honor, who had taken on responsibility for decorations, was also frustrated by the constant changes. I even heard whispers—though I cannot say for sure—that she was having second thoughts about continuing in that role.

Finally, out of sheer frustration, both my aunt and Mother Merle confronted Zuleika about her indecisiveness, telling her that her frequent adjustments were making it next to impossible to finalize plans. Rather than showing gratitude or humility, Zuleika lashed out. Her response was distasteful, riddled with curses, and dripping with disdain. In one shocking moment, she uninvited both my Aunt Peaches and Mother Merle—two women who had poured their time, love, and even financial support into helping make the day possible.

It was at this point that Mother Merle, the very same woman who had once encouraged me to move forward, looked at me and said something that has never left my memory: *"God can change His mind."*

This was someone I looked up to, someone I considered a spiritual mother. To hear her reversal shook me to the core. Her words forced me to confront the sobering reality that perhaps what I had believed to be God's will was not His will at all.

The wedding was supposed to mark a new beginning—a celebration of covenant, joy, and the sacred union that reflects Christ's love for His Church. But what unfolded was far from the hopeful vision I held.

# The Wedding Day: A Silent Collapse

The morning of the wedding, I woke up heavy. My body moved, but my spirit felt bound. I dressed carefully in a black suit with a crisp white shirt and a deep wine-colored tie—classic, sharp, and dignified. I wanted to look my best, even though my heart was unsettled.

I arrived at the church early, around 11:00 a.m., prepared for what should have been a joyous day. Roughly one hundred people gathered in the sanctuary—family, friends, the bridal party, and church members. The number would have been larger, but Zuleika had already excluded several people who had offended her in the weeks leading up to the wedding.

Then the waiting began. An hour passed. Then another. All told, I sat there for over two hours. The congregation shifted uncomfortably in their seats. Murmurs rippled through the room. Some people quietly excused themselves, unable to stay any longer. I sat at the front, humiliated, staring at the door and the clock, praying for strength just to sit still.

When Zuleika finally arrived, her entrance was not marked by humility or grace, but by arrogance. With an air of superiority, she unapologetically dismissed the entire ordeal with one phrase: *"Let him wait."* As if my time, my dignity, and the sacredness of the day meant nothing to her.

It wasn't only the lateness—it was the attitude. She carried herself as though she were the center of the universe, implying that I should have no problem waiting endlessly because she was "worth it." When pressed on why she had delayed so long, she sneered and repeated, *"Let him wait."*

Those words stung like a dagger. They stripped away the illusion and revealed her heart more clearly than any prayer or sermon could. This day was not about a covenant. It was not about Christ.

It was not about partnership. It was about power, control, and her need to be worshiped at the expense of everyone else.

As the bridal party entered, I was shocked by what she wore. Her dress was tight, revealing, and showed much more than I was comfortable with, especially in the context of a wedding tied to ministry. The cleavage was exposed, the fabric stretched to its limits—an open insult not only to me but to the very ministry I had hoped to build with her.

Zuleika was not physically what most would call the ideal bride, but her narcissistic voice proclaimed loudly, "I am the sexiest woman here." She sought attention and validation at every turn, and the dress was her weapon of choice.

When she reached the altar, tears flowed—not from happiness, but from deep sorrow and fear. I realized with a crushing certainty that I was about to make the biggest mistake of my life.

Weddings should be filled with joy, anticipation, and peace. Instead, I felt sadness, confusion, stress, anxiety, depression, and an overwhelming desire to run away.

Adding to this, I had previously asked to keep our public display of affection modest. I preferred no deep kiss in front of my parents, hoping to save that intimacy for later. Zuleika ignored my wishes completely and went all in, disregarding my boundaries and feelings.

"Above all, keep loving one another earnestly, since love covers a multitude of sins." (1 Peter 4:8)

"But everything should be done in a fitting and orderly way." (1 Corinthians 14:40)

Her actions were neither loving nor orderly—they were selfish and disruptive.

## The Moment of Truth

The pastor said the words, "You are now man and wife," and the moment should have been sacred and beautiful. Instead, Zuleika immediately declared, *"I wanted you, and I got you."*

Her words were chilling but truthful. She had wanted me, and she had done everything within her power—possibly even supernatural manipulation—to ensure this moment.

The weight of that statement crushed me. It was a declaration of possession, not partnership. I felt trapped in a cage built on manipulation, false hope, and spiritual confusion.

"Do you not know that to whom you present yourselves slaves to obey, you are that one's slaves whom you obey, whether of sin leading to death, or of obedience leading to righteousness?" (Romans 6:16)

I realized I was caught between two masters—one of spiritual truth and one of spiritual deception.

## The Spiritual Danger of False Prophecy and Witchcraft

Zuleika's family background included dark spiritual influences, including reported involvement in witchcraft. This was a reality I hadn't fully understood or confronted.

The unnatural intensity of desire I experienced after Zuleika's trip to Haiti, where she visited places connected to these spiritual practices, felt more like a spiritual binding than natural affection.

The suspicion I once brushed aside now loomed like an undeniable shadow.

The Bible teaches clearly about the spiritual battle raging around us:

"For we do not wrestle against flesh and blood, but against principalities, against powers, against the rulers of the darkness of this age, against spiritual hosts of wickedness in the heavenly places." (Ephesians 6:12)

God's Word warns us:

"Submit yourselves therefore to God. Resist the devil, and he will flee from you." (James 4:7)

"And no wonder, for Satan himself masquerades as an angel of light." (2 Corinthians 11:14)

This highlights the need for spiritual vigilance, especially when relationships intersect with dark spiritual activity.

## Lessons on Spiritual Discernment

Spiritual discernment is vital in all relationships, especially those claiming Christian faith. Too often, people use Scripture as a shield or sword to justify selfish behavior, control, or manipulation.

Be cautious when religious language is used to silence your concerns or to demand submission without love and respect.

"Love is patient and kind; love does not envy or boast; it is not arrogant or rude. It does not insist on its own way." (1 Corinthians 13: 4–5)

Zuleika's repeated claims of "doing this for God" were hollow without the fruit of love, patience, and humility.

The heart can deceive:

"The heart is deceitful above all things, and desperately sick; who can understand it?" (Jeremiah 17:9)

## Contemporary Examples: The Mask of Religious Manipulation

Spiritual manipulation disguised as religious duty is more common than we think.

Consider leaders who demand absolute obedience, dismissing dissent as sin, or spouses who use Scripture to control, shame, or silence their partners. These behaviors cause deep wounds and often go unaddressed due to fear, shame, or spiritual confusion.

"But encourage one another daily, as long as it is called 'Today,' so that none of you may be hardened by sin's deceitfulness." (Hebrews 3:13)

The Church must create safe spaces for honest conversations and healing.

## The Silent Surrender

By the wedding day, I was already surrendering silently—not surrendering in faith, but in confusion, pain, and the desperate desire to keep peace at any cost.

I lost my voice. Every time I wanted to speak up, I hesitated, worried about causing conflict or being labeled spiritually rebellious. At the altar, my silence deepened. During the vows, my silence bound me. During the kiss, my silence betrayed me. And when she declared, *"I wanted you, and I got you,"* my silence sealed me.

"Do not quench the Spirit. Do not despise prophecies, but test everything; hold fast what is good." (1 Thessalonians 5:19–21)

"Love is not rude, it does not insist on its own way." (1 Corinthians 13:5)

My silence was not submission to God—it was bondage. Yet even in silence and confusion, God's presence remained. Your voice may feel trapped now, but He is listening and preparing you to speak truth in His timing.

## Reflection: When Hope Becomes Heartache

"Hope deferred makes the heart sick." My hope for love, partnership, and a shared journey with God became delayed, twisted, and broken.

This is a warning for anyone walking through similar fires:

• Do not ignore your intuition or the red flags you see.

• Do not allow spiritual language to silence your pain or mute your voice.

• Be vigilant for false prophecy and manipulation hidden behind a mask of holiness.

• Seek God's truth with courage, and never settle for less than peace, respect, and mutual love.

"The LORD is close to the brokenhearted and saves those who are crushed in spirit." (Psalm 34:18)

"Trust in the LORD with all your heart and lean not on your own understanding; in all your ways submit to Him, and He will make your paths straight." (Proverbs 3:5–6)

Take comfort in knowing that discernment, courage, and God's presence guide your next steps.

## Prayer Starters – Chapter 3

• Lord, give me courage to speak truth in love, even when it is difficult.

• Father, open my eyes to spiritual deception and protect me from manipulation.

• Jesus, teach me to discern Your voice above all others.

• Holy Spirit, heal the wounds caused by broken promises and misguided hope.

• God, restore my voice, peace, and sense of direction.

## Reflection Questions – Chapter 3

• Have you ever experienced a moment when hope turned into heartache? How did you respond?

• How do you discern when spiritual language is being used to manipulate rather than guide?

• What boundaries can you establish to protect your heart and voice in relationships?

• How can the Church better support those caught in spiritual or emotional manipulation?

## Transition to Chapter 4

The wedding was over, but the real fire was just beginning. The vows I made in trembling silence would soon be tested in the furnace of daily life. What I thought was covenant turned into captivity, and the home I longed to build became a living Gehenna. Little did I know, the vows I made in silence would ignite a furnace I could not have imagined.

# Chapter 4 – The Prison of Peacekeeping

*"Blessed are the peacemakers, for they will be called children of God."* (Matthew 5:9)

—Understanding the difference between godly peace and toxic silence.

## A Reception to Remember—for All the Wrong Reasons

After the ceremony, we stepped out for photos. What should have been a brief, joyful interlude quickly spiraled into a frustrating, exhausting, and expensive ordeal. Zuleika lingered, directing photographers as if she were on a celebrity film set. Every instruction seemed endless. Every pause stretched the schedule. Every request for a retake felt like another added weight on my shoulders.

The photographers and videographers—originally hired for a specific time window—began charging overtime. Every additional minute added more stress and financial burden. Every glance at the clock felt like another blow. My chest tightened, my mind raced, and a creeping sense of panic began to rise.

*"Smile, Cordell. Just smile."* I forced my mouth into a grin while the camera clicked. My jaw ached from pretending. Inside, I was screaming: *"This isn't joy. This isn't a covenant. This is debt, stress, and humiliation dressed up as a wedding."*

I had already emptied my life savings to fund this wedding. The lavish dress, the decorated venue, airfare for her so-called "brother," and countless unexpected extras—all had come from my own pocket. Every dollar felt like a hard-fought sacrifice, yet now it seemed to crumble before my eyes.

Zuleika's response was simple optimism: *"The gifts from the guests will cover it."* But assuming is not planning. Optimism without preparation is still recklessness. Proverbs 21:5 reminds us:

*"The plans of the diligent lead surely to abundance, but everyone who is hasty comes only to poverty."*

As the minutes dragged on, my spirit grew heavier. What should have been a moment of joy and relief was replaced by gnawing unease, anxiety, and fear. My body grew tense, my hands shook slightly, and a deep sense of dread settled over me. Every smile I forced, every laugh I tried to conjure for the cameras, felt like a mask over my real feelings of worry and humiliation.

**Expanded Reflection:**

Even in small moments, our responses reveal much about the boundaries we set for ourselves. The temptation to appease, to smile through pain, can subtly imprison us before we even recognize it. I began to see that what I had thought was patience was turning into silent suffering. Like a bird trapped in a gilded cage, I had the appearance of freedom but none of the strength to fly.

# When the Murmuring Began

By the time we arrived at the reception, the energy in the room had shifted. Guests, who had once been bright-eyed and eager, now looked weary, hungry, and visibly irritated. Quiet whispers rippled through the crowd. Some frowned subtly, others glanced at their watches. A baby cried in the corner while an elderly church mother shook her head softly. The celebration had become charged with tension, and the joy that should have filled the room was replaced by an invisible heaviness.

*"They're whispering about me. They're wondering why I'm letting this happen. Why can't I just say something? Why am I frozen?"*

My chest felt tight, shame crawling up my throat. I felt like the whole room could see the war going on inside me.

I told myself, *"Hold it together. Don't ruin the night. Don't let this get out of hand."* But inside, I was unraveling.

James 1:19 instructs:

*"Let every person be quick to hear, slow to speak, slow to anger."*

But discernment without action can become passive complicity. I had chosen silence in the hope of avoiding conflict, but the cost was high: my dignity, my peace, and my emotional stability.

Proverbs 29:25 warns:

*"The fear of man will prove to be a snare, but whoever trusts in the Lord is kept safe."*

**Expanded Insight:**

Peacekeeping often masquerades as virtue, but the spiritual cost of avoiding confrontation can be immense. True peace aligns with righteousness; it does not silence conscience or honor.

## The First Dance from Hell

Then came the first dance—a moment that should have symbolized intimacy, covenant, and joy between husband and wife. Instead, it became a spectacle of humiliation.

Zuleika approached me not with tenderness or grace, but with provocation. She began gyrating, grinding, and laughing in a manner entirely inappropriate for the setting. The crowd watched, some shifting uncomfortably in their seats, others whispering, and a few openly staring.

I stood stiffly, frozen, humiliated. My body would not cooperate. My hands hung awkwardly at my sides. My face flushed with shame.

*"God, no... not here, not like this."* My mind screamed. *"I'm supposed to lead with dignity, but I feel like a clown on display. Lord, help me. How do I escape without exploding? How do I honor You when I feel mocked?"*

Romans 12:17–18 reminds us:

*"Repay no one evil for evil... If possible, so far as it depends on you, live peaceably with all."*

Yet true peace does not mean allowing open disrespect to dominate. Silence without courage, I realized, had become a form of bondage.

This was more than embarrassment; it was a challenge to everything I believed about marriage, honor, and covenant. My calling and ministry felt exposed, and I questioned whether I had misjudged the true nature of this union.

## A Disturbing Display

If that moment weren't enough, the man Zuleika insisted was her "brother"—for whom I had paid both a visa and airfare—became her next target. In front of the gathered crowd, she danced with him in the same provocative way, laughing, grinding, and mocking the vows we had just exchanged before God.

The guests were visibly uncomfortable. Some shifted in their seats, others lowered their eyes, and a few whispered in disbelief.

*"This is it. Everyone sees it now. The whispers I've tried to silence in my own head—about her past, about her loyalties—they're all being confirmed on this dance floor. She's laughing, but my spirit*

*is dying. Did I walk into a covenant or a cage? God, why did I ignore the warnings?"*

This was not just disrespect—it was desecration. A sacred covenant, established before God, was being mocked.

Psalm 34:19 reminds us:

*"Many are the afflictions of the righteous, but the Lord delivers him out of them all."*

Even in public humiliation and betrayal, God is near to deliver, guide, and restore.

## Peace or Passivity?

Why didn't I stop the music? Why didn't I confront the behavior? Why didn't I walk out?

Because I had become a prisoner of peacekeeping, I didn't want to create a scene. I didn't want to embarrass anyone—even while being humiliated myself. I had mistaken passivity for peacemaking.

Colossians 3:15 says:

*"Let the peace of Christ rule in your hearts."*

True peace is not passive or fear-driven; it is ruled by Christ and aligned with righteousness. I realized that my desire for calm had become a cage, trapping me in shame, humiliation, and fear. What I had considered keeping the peace was really fear disguised as virtue.

Ezekiel 13:10 warns:

*"They have seen false visions and lying divinations, saying, 'Peace,' when there is no peace."*

### Expanded Reflection:

God's peace demands courage. It allows confrontation when righteousness is threatened. False peace is comfortable, but its cost is often unseen until it crushes the soul.

## God's Peace vs. Man's

God's peace brings clarity, healing, and order. What I had experienced was counterfeit—a false calm demanding silence at the expense of truth.

Jesus warned in Matthew 10:34:

*"Do not suppose that I have come to bring peace to the earth. I did not come to bring peace, but a sword."*

Sometimes truth divides before it heals. False peace must be disrupted to allow God's real peace to reign.

John 16:33 reminds us:

*"In this world, you will have trouble. But take heart! I have overcome the world."*

Real peace is not the absence of difficulty—it is the presence of Christ in the midst of difficulty. I was not a peacemaker—I was being held hostage by shame, fear, and obligation. My silence was bondage, not strength.

# Final Straw, Not the Final Word

That night became a turning point. I could not unsee what had happened, nor could I pretend this was "just a rough start." God was peeling back layers of deception, revealing the chains I had walked under.

Yet His grace remained. Psalm 34:18 says:

*"The Lord is close to the brokenhearted and saves those who are crushed in spirit."*

This painful exposure was not the end—it was a beginning. It was a call to confront truth, set boundaries, and refuse the domination of false peace. Isaiah 61:3 promises:

*"...to grant to those who mourn in Zion—to give them a beautiful headdress instead of ashes..."*

Even humiliation can be transformed into testimony.

The reception lights dimmed, but the fire was only beginning to burn brighter. What started as public humiliation would soon become private torment. Behind closed doors, the applause faded, the guests disappeared, and the real furnace began to roar. The prison of peacekeeping had only been the doorway—what lay ahead was a Gehenna I could never have imagined.

# Chapter 5 – When Prayer Becomes Survival

*"The righteous cry, and the Lord heareth, and delivereth them out of all their troubles."*

(Psalm 34:17, KJV)

—Clinging to God when nothing else makes sense.

## When Trust is Shaken

The honeymoon—a season meant for sacred intimacy, emotional connection, and joyful beginnings—turned into an unexpected trial. I had pictured quiet mornings together, whispered prayers, laughter, and the sacred closeness of a couple beginning life as one.

Instead, Zuleika had made no arrangements for her so-called brother after the reception. In a twist I could not have anticipated, she left with him, and I was left to stay with family.

I kept asking myself: *Is this really how a honeymoon should be spent?* My heart was heavy, clouded with confusion, disappointment, and a deep sense of betrayal. Each day stretched long and uncertain. I wrestled with whether I could trust my wife again. My desire for intimacy waned—not out of rejection, but out of hurt, caution, and a deep need for emotional security.

When she returned to our matrimonial home after her brother left, the tension persisted. She was still on her menstrual cycle and insisted that we proceed with marital intimacy, citing the principle that the bed was "undefiled." I could not bring myself to act against my conscience. I felt strongly that this was a moment to wait, honoring both physical boundaries and spiritual integrity. I insisted on waiting, trusting that God's timing and guidance should govern the intimacy of our union.

The nights were quiet, almost unbearably so, yet they were filled with internal struggle. I lay awake, hands folded, eyes open in darkness, whispering prayers that were raw and unscripted:

*"Lord, guide me. Guard my heart. Show me how to respond with wisdom. Protect me from resentment, bitterness, and temptation."*

Psalm 34:17 became my anchor:

*"The righteous cry, and the Lord heareth, and delivereth them out of all their troubles."* (Psalm 34:17, KJV)

Every prayer became a thread holding me together, a channel to release my grief, disappointment, and questions to the One who sees all.

I followed the exhortation of Lamentations 2:19:

*"Arise, cry out in the night: in the beginning of the watches pour out thine heart like water before the face of the Lord: lift up thy hands toward him for the life of thy young children, that faint for hunger in the top of every street."* (Lamentations 2:19, KJV)

I poured out everything—pain, betrayal, hesitation, longing for guidance. In that act of honest surrender, I found that God began to show me the subtle contours of His wisdom. My prayers were no longer just survival—they became a dialogue of discernment, teaching me to wait patiently, to guard my heart, and to recognize that physical intimacy must always align with spiritual clarity and trust.

Each day, I observed Zuleika closely. Her attention was mostly on her own schedule, her body, and her social interactions, rather than on building spiritual intimacy in the home. Yet in my isolation, I found moments of divine clarity. I could pray without interruption, read Scripture without distraction, and quietly meditate on God's promises for marriage, patience, and discernment.

Even the simplest thoughts—like sitting in silence, reflecting on Ephesians 4:2–3—became exercises in self-control and spiritual endurance:

*"With all lowliness and meekness, with longsuffering, forbearing one another in love; Endeavouring to keep the unity of the Spirit in the bond of peace."* (Ephesians 4:2–3, KJV)

I realized that waiting was not passive; it was a spiritual discipline, a way of aligning my heart to God before engaging in the sacred act of marital intimacy.

In these days of tension, I journaled constantly. Every fear, every moment of doubt, every prayerful plea was recorded. The journal became a sacred witness to the internal conflict I had: the clash between desire for closeness and the need to honor God, the pain of betrayal, and the struggle to maintain hope.

## The First Weeks: Living in a Straitjacket

The days following the honeymoon felt like entering a prison I had not anticipated. Our matrimonial home, which should have been a sanctuary, felt heavy and suffocating. Every movement I made seemed observed, critiqued, or corrected. I was walking on eggshells, acutely aware that a single misstep could trigger a conflict.

Zuleika spent most of her time on the phone, laughing, whispering, and making plans with friends while I remained physically present but emotionally absent. Her attention was rarely on our relationship, leaving me isolated, trapped, and unsure how to connect. My body ached with loneliness, and my spirit felt restrained, as if invisible chains bound me to a constant state of vigilance.

Every attempt at conversation was met with minimal engagement. Her tone was curt or dismissive, and I began to feel the weight of invisibility pressing down on me. Even in silence, I was hyper-aware of her presence—every glance, movement, and sigh felt loaded with judgment. My home, which should have offered comfort, became a place of tension and exhaustion.

Psalm 27:1 became my anchor:

*"The Lord is my light and my salvation; whom shall I fear? the Lord is the strength of my life; of whom shall I be afraid?"* (Psalm 27:1, KJV)

I clung to this promise daily, whispering it as I moved through the house, seeking divine reassurance in the midst of relational oppression.

## Two Weeks After Our Wedding

Two weeks after our wedding, Zuleika and I had an appointment scheduled for 11 a.m. that morning. I had also promised to give my mom a ride to go shopping. I was juggling both, trying to keep the peace. But by noon, Zuleika was still asleep, and it was getting late. By 1 p.m., I decided I couldn't wait any longer. I was going to leave without her.

In response, she hid the car keys. I didn't want to escalate things, so I decided I'd just walk the 4.5 miles to my appointment. It wasn't ideal, but I'd deal with it.

Later that evening, my phone rang. It was Zuleika. My stomach sank when I heard her voice.

"I'm in an accident," she said.

I felt like the ground shifted beneath me. I asked her where and what happened, thinking she was in a bus or a cab, maybe trying to get to me. But she said she was fine. It was my car.

I couldn't believe it. She'd taken my Ford Explorer—the car that's known for being tough as nails—and gone to my aunt's house, then headed to the shopping area. On the way, she drove through a school zone just before school let out and hit five or more cars. The damage was bad.

I immediately started running to her. The area wasn't the safest— gangs, guns, all of it—but I wasn't going to leave her there.

When I got close, I saw a man yelling at her. He was furious, shouting about how he wanted to kill her. "Someone bring my [expletive] gun! I'm putting a bullet in her head!"

I was already on edge, but I couldn't lose my temper. I stepped in calmly. "It doesn't have to go that far. I've got insurance. I'll pay for a rental car for you. Let's just get through this."

The man's BMW was wrecked, but I kept my cool, even as he raged. Just when I thought things couldn't get worse, another guy appeared—out of nowhere—and told the angry man, "Leave her alone. It's just metal. It can be fixed."

I didn't know where he came from or where he went, but in that moment, I felt like he was sent by God.

The situation was tense. I pulled Zuleika aside and told her to act hurt, hoping we could get out of there without things getting worse. I called an ambulance before the cops arrived.

At the hospital, the cops came in, trying to question her. I told her, "Don't answer anything." She looked scared, and I could tell she wasn't processing what was happening. Eventually, the officers left, but the days that followed were tough. Zuleika started acting like a baby, pretending to be sick, avoiding responsibility for her actions.

I didn't throw it in her face. I didn't yell or make her feel worse. But I was frustrated. I asked her gently, "What were you thinking when you took the car? You didn't have a permit, a license, or any driving experience."

Her answer made my blood run cold. "I just wanted to surprise you."

Surprise me? By completely upending our lives just two weeks after we got married and becoming a liability?

I was angry, but deep down, I still tried to be supportive. I didn't want to throw it in her face, even though I felt like she'd put me in a terrible position. As a husband, I wanted to be there for her, to help her, but this was a lot.

And the aftermath? Getting auto insurance after that accident? It was a nightmare. The payout from that mess made everything harder.

## Spiritual Solitude and the Weight of Prayer

In this environment, prayer became my refuge. I found myself seeking God's presence in the quietest corners of the house: kneeling at the edge of the bed, sitting quietly, or pacing in the kitchen. These moments were both draining and essential.

I prayed for strength to endure the emotional weight, for clarity in discerning Zuleika's intentions, and for guidance in responding with wisdom rather than anger. The isolation forced me to rely entirely on God, and I whispered Scripture into the shadows of the home, claiming verses as lifelines:

- *"God is our refuge and strength, a very present help in trouble."* (Psalm 46:1, KJV)
- *"Fear thou not; for I am with thee: be not dismayed; for I am thy God: I will strengthen thee; yea, I will help thee; yea, I will uphold thee with the right hand of my righteousness."* (Isaiah 41:10, KJV)

Though physically alone, these prayers reminded me that I was never spiritually abandoned. I began to see the house not as a prison, but as a place where my faith could be tested, refined, and strengthened.

## Nights of Prayer: Expanding the Narrative

**Night 1:** I knelt at the side of the bed, chest tight with anxiety, whispering fragments of Psalms. My mind raced through fears, regrets, and questions. I noticed a subtle trembling in my hands as I prayed aloud: "Lord, give me clarity. Help me not to fear the silence or the emptiness." That night, a profound sense of God's presence washed over me, quieting my restless thoughts.

**Night 2:** Sitting quietly in the living room, shadows stretching across the room, I prayed for discernment, asking God to reveal the motivations behind every word and action I observed. As I prayed, I realized I was not simply longing for comfort—I was learning to rely fully on God's wisdom rather than my own instincts.

**Night 3:** Pacing the kitchen, I poured out grief that I hadn't even fully acknowledged to myself. Tears came silently as I spoke to God about betrayal and unmet expectations. I felt a strange mix of relief and exhaustion. That night, the Scripture from Lamentations 2:19 echoed in my heart:

*"Arise, cry out in the night: in the beginning of the watches pour out thine heart like water before the face of the Lord: lift up thy*

*hands toward him for the life of thy young children, that faint for hunger in the top of every street."* (Lamentations 2:19, KJV)

I understood the power of unfiltered honesty in prayer.

**Night 4:** Kneeling by the living room window, I reflected on my role in this marriage, asking God to align my actions with His will. I wrestled with feelings of guilt, questioning whether my restraint was misinterpreted as weakness. I felt a whisper of assurance: *"Your patience is not in vain."*

**Night 5:** On the fifth night, I journaled for hours, documenting every emotion, every prayer, every thought. I recognized patterns of fear and hope interwoven, and the journal became a sanctuary for reflection. God's quiet confirmations through Scripture brought subtle peace even amidst the ongoing trials.

**Night 6:** I turned my focus to gratitude, recalling God's faithfulness in past trials. I read Psalms 23 and 34 aloud, meditating on each verse. My prayer became less about seeking relief and more about acknowledging God's provision, even in relational tension. I felt a shift in my heart—a gentle reminder that survival in prayer includes not only asking but also thanking.

*"The Lord is my shepherd; I shall not want. He maketh me to lie down in green pastures: he leadeth me beside the still waters. He restoreth my soul: he leadeth me in the paths of righteousness for his name's sake."* (Psalm 23:1–3, KJV)

**Night 7:** On the seventh night, I prayed for endurance, imagining the strength of biblical figures who survived betrayal and isolation through prayer. Hannah, David, and even Jesus in Gethsemane came to mind. I whispered a prayer of surrender: "Lord, take my fears, my expectations, my pain, and make them holy in Your hands."

*"Cast thy burden upon the Lord, and he shall sustain thee: he shall never suffer the righteous to be moved."* (Psalm 55:22, KJV)

I realized that each night of prayer was teaching me a different dimension of spiritual survival: honesty, discernment, patience, reflection, gratitude, surrender, and dependence on God. The process was transforming me from the inside out, showing me that even when human companionship falls short, God's presence is more than enough.

## The Struggle for Emotional and Spiritual Integrity

Each day, I wrestled internally with competing desires. I longed for marital closeness, partnership, and emotional connection—but I also needed to honor God, my conscience, and the boundaries I believed were essential for our marriage to flourish.

The tension between expectation and reality left me exhausted. I questioned myself constantly:

- Am I overreacting?
- Should I confront her?
- Is my need for personal space selfish?

In these moments, I returned to 1 Corinthians 10:13:

*"There hath no temptation taken you but such as is common to man: but God is faithful, who will not suffer you to be tempted above that ye are able; but will with the temptation also make a way to escape, that ye may be able to bear it."* (1 Corinthians 10:13, KJV)

My patience, restraint, and discernment were becoming acts of spiritual endurance rather than weakness. I learned that endurance is not simply waiting—it is active reliance on God, a spiritual muscle strengthened by every prayer, every journal entry, and every conscious choice to honor God above human expectation.

# Clinging to God's Word in Isolation

Though Zuleika rarely prayed in the home—reading a Psalm only occasionally and superficially—my time in prayer became transformative. Each session was a chance to:

- Pour out grief and betrayal (Lamentations 2:19)
- Seek divine wisdom for navigating relational tension
- Affirm God's presence even when human partnership failed

I journaled every day, documenting moments of temptation, doubt, or emotional fatigue, and recording God's responses through Scripture or sudden clarity. These journals became sacred witnesses to my struggle, a roadmap of spiritual survival during a season where human support was absent.

## Reflection Points

1. How do you navigate intimacy and trust when emotional or relational boundaries have been challenged?
2. How can prayer guide you in situations where physical closeness is complicated by emotional tension or hesitation?
3. When has God asked you to wait on Him before proceeding with a decision, even in moments of expectation or pressure?
4. How do you maintain spiritual vigilance when those closest to you are spiritually distant?
5. How can journaling or focused prayer become tools for endurance in relational tension?

## Prayer Starters

- Lord, sustain me when human support is absent.
- Father, give me strength to maintain integrity under emotional pressure.
- Holy Spirit, guard my heart from bitterness and despair.
- Jesus, help me see Your presence in the silent moments.
- God, teach me to rely fully on You, even when earthly partnership is lacking.

## Practical Action Guide – Walking Through Emotional and Spiritual Trials

### Step 1: Establish Sacred Spaces for Prayer

- Reflect: Identify areas where you can commune with God privately.
- Action: Create a daily prayer routine, even for short, focused sessions.
- Scripture: *"He that dwelleth in the secret place of the most High shall abide under the shadow of the Almighty."* (Psalm 91:1, KJV)

### Step 2: Document Spiritual Encounters

- Reflect: Record prayers, reflections, and moments of divine clarity.
- Action: Journal daily, noting God's guidance, scripture impressions, and emotional breakthroughs.
- Scripture: *"Write the vision, and make it plain upon tables, that he may run that readeth it."* (Habakkuk 2:2, KJV)

## Step 3: Guard Emotional Boundaries

- Reflect: Identify moments where emotional overextension may harm spiritual clarity.
- Action: Set intentional boundaries to protect your heart while maintaining openness to God.
- Scripture: *"Keep thy heart with all diligence; for out of it are the issues of life."* (Proverbs 4:23, KJV)

## Step 4: Seek Divine Perspective Before Human Confrontation

- Reflect: Pause before responding to tension or disrespect.
- Action: Pray for wisdom and clarity before speaking, ensuring responses align with godly principles.
- Scripture: *"If any of you lack wisdom, let him ask of God, that giveth to all men liberally, and upbraideth not; and it shall be given him."* (James 1:5, KJV)

## Step 5: Practice Patience and Waiting

- Reflect: Spiritual endurance is strengthened by waiting.
- Action: Choose to wait on God's timing in relational decisions and marital intimacy.
- Scripture: *"Wait on the Lord: be of good courage, and he shall strengthen thine heart: wait, I say, on the Lord."* (Psalm 27:14, KJV)

## Step 6: Celebrate Small Victories in Faith

- Reflect: Notice moments where prayer brings peace or clarity.
- Action: Record each small breakthrough to remind yourself of God's faithfulness.
- Scripture: *"Be careful for nothing; but in every thing by prayer and supplication with thanksgiving let your requests be made known unto God. And the peace of God, which passeth all understanding, shall keep your hearts and minds through Christ Jesus."* (Philippians 4:6–7, KJV)

# Chapter 6 – The Isolation of the Pit

"No one came to my support, but the Lord stood by my side." (2 Timothy 4:16–17, KJV)

—Experiencing emotional abandonment and discovering God's presence.

## Entering the Pit

The first weeks of my marriage felt as though I had been dropped into a deep, confining pit—a place of darkness, suffocating oppression, and endless emotional trials.

Life in the house was not companionship; it was a rigid exercise in control and dominance. Every morning, I awoke to the silence of her sleeping form, knowing that I could not make a sound. No television, no radio, no music.

Even my movements had to be careful, measured, and invisible. I tiptoed as though walking on eggshells, holding my breath until she woke.

When she did rise, often not until high noon, the world immediately shifted to revolve around her comfort and desires. I had no voice in her schedule, no ability to establish normal routines, and no space to feel like a husband. Every movement I made, every thought I tried to share, was either scrutinized or dismissed. Even the simplest suggestion or observation was met with disdain or silence.

We exchanged words, but these were not conversations; they were fleeting exchanges, rarely lasting more than a few minutes, and often ending in subtle arguments or curt dismissals. I felt invisible, confined, and trapped, as though the walls themselves were closing in on me. This was not the companionship I had imagined in marriage; it was a straitjacket, suppressing my voice, limiting my freedom, and constricting my spirit.

I began to dread going home after work. Instead of longing for the sanctuary of my own house, I found myself lingering outside as long as possible, stalling for time before walking through the door. Home was no longer a refuge; it was a place of suffocating tension.

Scriptural Anchors:

- Psalm 40:2 – "He lifted me out of the slimy pit, out of the mud and mire; he set my feet on a rock and gave me a firm place to stand."
- Even when trapped in circumstances that feel hopeless, God provides a firm foundation for those who cry to Him. My pit felt real, yet He was preparing a secure footing beneath my weary spirit.
- Deuteronomy 31:6 – "Be strong and courageous. Do not be afraid or terrified…for the Lord your God goes with you; he will never leave you nor forsake you."
- Courage is not the absence of fear but reliance on God's steadfast presence. Even in total isolation, I learned to lean into His promises.

**Mini Devotional Break:**

Think about a time you felt trapped or unseen. How did God show His presence in that moment? Could this have been a test of endurance and trust?

# The Weight of Abandonment

It quickly became clear that asserting myself was not tolerated. She insisted on having the final say in every matter, openly stating that I was not her head and would never be a governing authority in our marriage. Every disagreement was met with blunt verbal attacks:

she would insist I did not know anything, that I lacked understanding, and that my opinion was worthless.

The constant dismissal and undermining began to erode my sense of self. Even when I attempted to engage, the brief conversations often ended in tension or irritation. I longed for moments of laughter, mutual care, or simple companionship—but such moments were fleeting or nonexistent.

Zuleika also began limiting who I could talk with, even among my closest family members. Every phone call was scrutinized, every conversation interrogated. She demanded to know every detail of what was said, where I was, and who I had been with. The walls of isolation closed in tighter with every passing day.

One night, overwhelmed by the pressure, I reached out to a cousin—someone I grew up with, who was more like a brother to me. I just needed someone I trusted, someone to vent my feelings to privately. But Zuleika overheard and erupted in rage, accusing me of sleeping with my own cousin. The accusation cut deep, both insulting and absurd, yet revealing just how twisted the atmosphere of distrust had become.

This type of behavior became daily life. My world shrank smaller and smaller, my voice quieter, my hope thinner. I realized I was no longer just in a bad marriage—I was in spiritual warfare.

I felt trapped, emasculated, and invisible in what should have been my home. The mental and emotional weight was almost unbearable. Anger, doubt, confusion, and despair became my constant companions. I wrestled with the question of whether I would ever experience peace, respect, or affirmation in this space.

Scriptural Anchors:

- Psalm 142:3 – "When my spirit grows faint within me, it is you who watch over my way."

- Even in emotional abandonment, God's watchful eye remains. I could pour out my spirit honestly, knowing He was present.
- Isaiah 41:13 – "For I am the Lord your God who takes hold of your right hand and says to you, Do not fear; I will help you."
- God's guidance is personal and intimate. In moments of despair, His hand steadied me, even when human support was absent.

**Reflection Exercise:**

Journal your feelings of isolation. Then, beside each entry, write a scripture that gives you hope or perspective.

# Spiritual Survival in the Silence

Amid the isolation, my faith became my only refuge. Prayer was no longer optional—it was survival. Each whispered plea, each kneeling session, became a lifeline, connecting me to God's presence. Even as confusion, doubt, and anger threatened to overwhelm me, I knew I could turn to Him.

I immersed myself in scripture, meditating on the stories of God's people in trial. I reflected on the Israelites, enslaved for 430 years, crying out for freedom. I found myself pleading with God to remember me, to guide my steps, and to bring clarity to my heart. In these moments, I recognized that this trial, though intense, was not beyond God's purview.

The isolation felt almost orchestrated by Satan himself, as though I had been singled out for spiritual testing. Yet I refused to surrender hope.

Psalm 34:17 became my anchor:

"The righteous cry out, and the Lord hears them."

Lamentations 2:19 guided me to release my emotions:

"Pour out your heart like water before the Lord."

I admitted my grief, anger, and confusion, pleading with God for discernment: when to forgive, when to trust, when to endure, and when to act.

**Prayer as Anchor:**

"Lord, I feel isolated, unseen, and worn down. Be my companion. Strengthen my heart and mind. Protect my spirit. Let me trust You fully, even when my world feels upside down. Grant me endurance, and let my faith remain unshaken."

# Emotional and Psychological Struggle

The continuous neglect, insults, and verbal assaults took a toll on my confidence. I began to walk with my head hung low—a stark contrast to the proud posture I had held even through poverty during my youth. I felt emasculated, diminished, and uncertain of my worth. Trust became a scarce commodity; I grew suspicious of everyone around me.

The temptation to leave was ever-present. I longed to vanish, to escape the scrutiny and oppression, to disappear entirely. Yet I recognized the danger in such an action—her vindictive nature meant running away could escalate conflict rather than resolve it. I chose endurance, leaning fully on God's timing, strength, and guidance.

Sometimes I was so overwhelmed with the problems that I didn't stop to hear what God was saying to me. My prayers became cries for survival more than moments of clarity. Yet even in that silence, I knew God was near, waiting patiently for me to listen.

Scriptural Anchors:

- Isaiah 55:8-9 – "For my thoughts are not your thoughts, neither are your ways my ways, declares the Lord."
- Psalm 27:1 – "The Lord is my light and my salvation—whom shall I fear? The Lord is the stronghold of my life—of whom shall I be afraid?"

**Mini Devotional Break:**

Isolation can feel like a test of identity. How does trusting God reshape your sense of self in trials?

# Lessons from the Pit

Living through this isolation revealed profound spiritual and personal truths:

1. God's Timing is Perfect: His deliverance may not align with human expectations, but it is always precise.
2. Faith Must Be Active: When human support is absent, prayer, scripture, and devotion sustain the soul.
3. Deliverance Requires Perseverance: Endurance in loneliness and oppression prepares the heart for victory.
4. God Can Be Trusted in Isolation: Even when no one stands beside you, God's presence never fails.
5. Spiritual Strength Grows in Trials: Each challenge deepens reliance on Him and builds resilience.

Scriptural Anchors:

- James 1:2-4 – "Consider it pure joy...whenever you face trials of many kinds, because you know that the testing of your faith produces perseverance."
- 2 Corinthians 12:9 – "My grace is sufficient for you, for my power is made perfect in weakness."

**Lesson Learned:** Even in abandonment, isolation, and misunderstanding, God's presence never departs. Enduring trials with prayer, scripture, and unwavering trust in His timing fosters spiritual growth and preserves integrity.

## Finding Strength and Hope

Even in the darkness, I discovered light. Prayer became my sanctuary; scripture, my sustenance; reflection, my path to clarity. I realized that deliverance begins with trust, even when the outcome is unseen.

Every day, I reminded myself: God's timing is perfect, His plans are higher than mine, and His faithfulness never wavers. This season of isolation, though painful, revealed God's sustaining power and His ability to carry me through trials that seemed insurmountable.

Scriptural Anchors:

- Psalm 23:4 – "Even though I walk through the valley of the shadow of death, I will fear no evil, for you are with me; your rod and your staff, they comfort me."
- Hebrews 13:5 – "Never will I leave you; never will I forsake you."

**Prayer Point:**

"Father, even when I feel unseen and abandoned, help me cling fully to You. Strengthen my faith, sustain my hope, and guide me through this trial. Teach me endurance, patience, and unwavering trust in Your perfect plan."

# Seven Nights of Prayer in the Pit

### Night 1: Crying Out in the Darkness

I knelt quietly in my room, chest heavy, whispering Psalm 34:17. Tears flowed freely as I admitted my pain, isolation, and confusion. I poured out everything to God, asking Him to guard my heart against bitterness and despair.

### Night 2: Seeking Discernment

I focused on understanding the situation, asking God to reveal the truth behind every tension. I prayed for wisdom in how to act, when to speak, and how to endure with integrity.

### Night 3: Releasing Anger and Grief

I acknowledged my anger, disappointment, and sense of betrayal. Lamentations 2:19 guided my prayer. I confessed all my raw emotions to God, feeling a release of tension I could not have found alone.

### Night 4: Strengthening Trust in God

I meditated on Psalm 27:1, repeating it softly. This night was about reminding myself that God's protection was constant, even when human support was absent.

### Night 5: Surrendering Control

I admitted my desire to escape, to fix, to control the situation, and surrendered it all to God. I acknowledged that His timing, not mine, would bring deliverance.

### Night 6: Gratitude Amid the Trial

Despite the pain, I remembered God's past faithfulness. Gratitude softened my spirit and allowed me to see the subtle ways God was sustaining me.

### Night 7: Commitment to Endurance

I committed myself to spiritual endurance. I prayed for patience, perseverance, and unwavering trust. I whispered:

"Lord, help me remain steadfast. Let my faith not waver. Teach me to see Your presence in every shadow, Your guidance in every challenge, and Your victory in every trial."

By the end of these seven nights, I realized that survival in the pit was not about avoiding pain—it was about deepening reliance on God, refining character, and anchoring my spirit in His Word.

## Spiritual Practices for Survival

- **Anchor in Prayer:** Speak openly to God about struggles, doubts, fears, and hopes.
- **Immerse in Scripture:** Study stories of endurance, faith, and God's faithfulness.
- **Journal Daily:** Record emotional struggles, spiritual insights, and answered prayers.
- **Endure Patiently:** Trust God's timing and remain steadfast in faith, knowing deliverance is near.
- **Reflect Continuously:** Take moments to identify growth, recognize answered prayers, and give God glory for sustaining you.

## Reflection Questions

1. How do you respond when human support is absent?
2. What scriptures bring you peace in isolation?
3. How can journaling help process emotional pain?
4. How does trusting God in a trial shape your sense of self?
5. What spiritual disciplines can you adopt to endure relational tension?
6. How can prayer become your lifeline when loneliness feels overwhelming?

## Transition to Chapter 7

The pit of isolation was deep, but it was only preparing me for an even sharper trial—the sting of false accusations. If isolation stripped me of companionship, the next season would threaten to rob me of reputation, integrity, and even identity.

# Chapter 7 – False Accusations, True Identity

"You intended to harm me, but God intended it for good." (Genesis 50:20, KJV)

—Facing false accusations while discovering the unshakable truth of God's purpose in your life.

## The Day It All Began

The day it all began, my life was thrown into chaos. Zuleika's behavior had escalated quickly, even after landing a very good job in my field. Before I had even received my first paycheck, she began spending recklessly.

One morning, while getting ready for work, I discovered she had hidden my car keys. Fear and tension immediately surged. We had a heated argument, and I was genuinely afraid of what she might do next.

In my fear, I called 911. While I was on the phone with the operator, Zuleika, who was in another room, overheard me. She immediately dialed 911 as well and began crying, claiming I was trying to kill her. The operator, hearing her on the line, informed responding officers that she suspected Zuleika was mentally unstable. When the police arrived, fearing she might hurt herself or someone else, they transported her to the hospital.

Meanwhile, unbeknownst to me, she began plotting her next move. By the time I returned home from work, the locks to our apartment had been changed. Without my knowledge, she had already obtained an order of protection against me. I was left with nothing—no documents, no personal belongings, only the clothes on my back.

I called my pastor and his wife, asking if they could help me get clothes for work. They were unable to reach her, only advising me that I should not attempt to be there.

Later that same week, the police arrived at the home of my relatives, where I had been staying. They had a warrant for my arrest. I asked on what grounds, and they inquired if I knew Zuleika. I had not spoken to her since leaving the apartment for work that morning. The officers explained that she had an order of protection against me and claimed I had tried to contact her—a statement that was false. I had not reached out to her in any way.

My elderly grandfather was present during this encounter, and I requested the officers not to handcuff me in front of him, asking instead that it be done outside.

## Arrest and Booking

While being taken in for booking, the officers advised me that I did not have to speak, but they expressed concern that Zuleika might be "up to no good" and suggested I keep as far away from her as possible.

My pastor soon arrived at the police station, invoking clergy-penitent privilege to see and speak with me. His words were brief, but I found no real comfort in them—he simply said, "God is going to get you through."

Because this was my first time being arrested, the sergeant could have issued a desk bail, releasing me without the full booking procedure. Instead, he was cold and procedural, choosing not to. After booking, I knew the next step would involve retaining a lawyer and appearing before the judge.

I felt a mix of disbelief, fear, and frustration. The cold formality of the legal system could not see the truth I knew in my heart. Yet in that moment, I had to cling to the reality that God's perspective is higher than man's.

## The First Family Court Hearing

The morning of the first family court hearing was tense. The courthouse towered above the streets, and each step I took echoed with anticipation. Inside, the family courtroom was smaller but heavy with formality. Clerks recorded my name and case number as I approached. My hands rested on my briefcase, my palms clammy, my heart racing.

Zuleika did not have to appear at this stage. The judge addressed procedural matters: reviewing filings, confirming service, and establishing a timeline for future family court hearings. My lawyer presented the sequence of events in writing: the hidden car keys, 911 calls, hospital transport, changed locks, and the wrongful order of protection. I observed quietly, aware that every detail mattered.

The judge set dates for upcoming hearings and confirmed that both parties would need to submit additional documentation. The weight of the future pressed on me, yet I leaned on prayer and Scripture to stay grounded:

- *Psalm 34:18 – "The LORD is near to the brokenhearted and saves the crushed in spirit."*
- *Psalm 23:4 – "Even though I walk through the valley of the shadow of death, I will fear no evil, for You are with me."*

## The Criminal Court Hearing

Not long after, the criminal hearing followed. The courthouse was a living machine—doors slamming, heels clicking, whispers echoing off the walls. Every sound felt amplified, reminding me how small I was in the eyes of the legal system.

I waited outside the judge's chambers, pacing the corridor. My mind raced with memories of Zuleika's accusations and the events that had led to this moment. My heart pounded like a drum, the tension almost physical. I whispered a prayer:

*"Lord, grant me patience. Grant me wisdom. Let Your truth shine through this darkness."*

When my name was called, I walked to the podium. The courtroom was sterile, the air heavy. There were no witnesses, no testimonies—only the case filed against me. The judge reviewed the paperwork, noting that Zuleika was not present. Bail was set at $10,000, but I was released on my own recognizance. Though physically free, I knew the battle was far from over.

## Courtroom Escalation – Molestation Accusation

Initially, Zuleika accused me of trying to drown her during a trip. The judge, skeptical, asked, "If that were true, why did you continue living with him?" Her credibility began to crumble, and the case seemed poised for dismissal.

In desperation, however, she blurted out that I had sexually molested her daughter. The accusation stunned the courtroom and froze everyone in disbelief. The judge could not dismiss it outright, so the case was continued pending investigation.

When her daughter was questioned, she courageously told the truth: her mother was lying and only wanted to get me in trouble. She did not want to speak to her mother. By this time, the daughter had been placed in foster care due to her mother's abuse: she had been slapped across the face, given bloody noses, made to stand in a corner for long periods, and forced to kneel on uncooked rice. The very person trying to destroy me was revealed as the true abuser.

# Days and Weeks After the Hearing

The days following the hearing were filled with tension, fear, and careful preparation. I lived at my relatives' home, surrounded by familiar walls that offered comfort yet reminded me of impermanence. Every lock clicking, every siren, every fluorescent light brought back memories of the arrest and booking.

Family support was limited but vital. My grandfather's quiet worry, my pastor's sparse counsel, and my lawyer's guidance were anchors. Most parishioners were sympathetic, often offering encouragement and prayer. Yet, I could feel unspoken doubts in the air—some who were close to me seemed to quietly wonder if I might be guilty. Their silence carried its own weight, and it pierced me almost as deeply as the accusations themselves.

The financial and practical strain was relentless. Lawyers had to be paid, and money drained quickly. Sleepless nights became normal. My body was present in bed, but my mind was restless—constantly replaying events, preparing for court, imagining scenarios. At times, I felt like I had to look over my shoulder wherever I went, always braced for another blow. Work suffered; I missed days from my job, and the stress bled into every aspect of my life.

And then there was the psychological weight. I found myself questioning my sanity. Could I really be losing my mind? But deep down, I never once believed the lies. I knew I was being set up. That truth anchored me, even as the storm raged.

My prayers became raw:

*"Why me, Lord? Is this storm going to pass?"*

In those moments, I felt as though God was silent. His silence was heavy, almost unbearable. But even in His silence, I never doubted that He had a greater purpose to fulfill through all of this.

There were moments of encouragement. Many people saw through Zuleika's lies, recognizing them for what they were. Their quiet acknowledgment of my innocence did not erase the pain, but it gave me glimpses of vindication that strengthened me to press forward.

Each night, I prayed:

*"Lord, protect me from despair. Guard my heart and my family. Strengthen me to face each court hearing with clarity, courage, and truth."*

I clung to Scripture as armor, repeating verses silently to steady my spirit:

- *Psalm 34:17 – "The righteous cry out, and the LORD hears them; he delivers them from all their troubles."*
- *Isaiah 54:17 – "No weapon formed against you shall prosper."*
- *Philippians 4:13 – "I can do all things through Christ who strengthens me."*

## Lessons and Practical Applications

Through these trials, I discovered spiritual and practical truths that can guide anyone facing false accusations or intense relational stress:

1. **Anchor in Scripture:** Memorize and meditate on verses that affirm God's protection, truth, and justice.
2. **Document Carefully:** Keep detailed records of events, communications, and evidence; clarity preserves integrity.
3. **Rely on Trusted Support:** Seek guidance from spiritual leaders, family, or counsel who see truth clearly.
4. **Maintain Faith-Focused Perspective:** Even when human systems fail, God's judgment and timing are perfect.

5. **Practical Preparedness:** Prepare for legal and emotional challenges by planning, reflecting, and praying daily.

## Affirmation of Faith

Though Zuleika's accusations had upended my life, led to my arrest, and brought me face-to-face with the cold procedures of the legal system, my identity remained intact. The weeks of fear, preparation, and prayer fortified me, reminding me that truth and faith were unshakable.

The battle was not over—the family court hearings loomed ahead—but I had emerged from the initial storm with resilience, grounded in Scripture, fortified by prayer, supported by family and parishioners, and secure in the knowledge that God alone knows the truth.

*"Lord, let Your truth shine. Let my life reflect Your justice and mercy. Strengthen me for the battles ahead."*

## Reflection Questions

1. How have false accusations or misunderstandings in your life challenged your faith and sense of identity?
2. When faced with fear and uncertainty, how can Scripture anchor your heart?
3. What personal habits or practices help you maintain clarity and composure in high-pressure situations?
4. In moments of isolation or when God seems silent, how do you continue to trust His purpose?
5. How can documenting events and reflecting on details be used as a tool for maintaining integrity and perspective?

## Prayer Starters

- Lord, help me to stand firm in truth even when others doubt me.
- Father, protect my heart and mind from fear, anger, and despair.
- God, give me clarity, wisdom, and courage as I navigate difficult situations.
- Lord, when You feel silent, help me to remember that You are still working for my good.
- Father, guide me through every challenge, and let Your justice and mercy prevail in my life.

## Transition into Chapter 8

Though I had endured the sting of false accusations, the cold machinery of the legal system, and the whispers of doubt from those around me, I knew my journey was far from finished. The accusations had scarred my reputation and shaken my foundation, but they had not destroyed me. In many ways, they had only revealed the depth of God's sustaining power.

Yet the trials ahead would not only test my faith in the courtroom—they would press into every corner of my life. What came next was not simply about surviving accusations but about confronting the spiritual battle that raged in the unseen, where lies, manipulation, and oppression collided with truth, endurance, and God's deliverance.

And so, as Chapter 8 unfolds, I step further into the fire—bound but not broken.

# Chapter 8 – Bound But Not Broken

*"We are hard pressed on every side, but not crushed; perplexed, but not in despair; persecuted, but not abandoned; struck down, but not destroyed."* —2 Corinthians 4:8–9

## The Weight of the Chains

Mornings felt like climbing a mountain I could not see the top of. My chest pressed down as if gravity itself had grown heavier overnight. The lies, the false accusations, the threats—they pressed on me from every direction. Each bill on the kitchen counter was a brick, each court summons a chain. Four criminal cases. One family case. Thousands of dollars I didn't have, demanded in a system that moved slowly, deliberately, to wear me down.

Yet, through it all, God sustained me. I still had work to do. I still had faith to walk in. I was bound by circumstances, pressed by accusations, hemmed in by systems that seemed designed to crush me—but I was not broken.

Even the air in my home felt thick with tension. Simple tasks—pouring a cup of coffee, opening the mailbox—became exercises in vigilance. Each phone call could carry bad news. Each knock at the door could be another demand. My spirit grew weary, but I reminded myself:

*"God's strength is made perfect in weakness"* (2 Corinthians 12:9).

## The First Arrest – Shock and Confusion

The knock on my relatives' door was sharp, final, and chilling. Two uniformed officers entered, badges gleaming, their presence carrying the weight of authority and presumption.

"Are you Zuleika's husband?" one asked. My heart sank. "No, I haven't contacted her," I replied, keeping my voice steady despite the rising panic.

They explained she had claimed I violated an order of protection. My elderly grandfather, seated silently nearby, looked on with worry etched across his face. I whispered to the officers, "Please, not in front of him," requesting the handcuffs be applied outside. They complied, but the cold efficiency of the procedure felt like a personal blow.

At the precinct, the sergeant noted that I could have been released at the desk, but instead followed full booking procedures. Hours dragged on. My pastor arrived, invoking clergy-penitent privilege to speak with me. His words were brief: "God is going to get you through." They were well-intentioned but did little to quiet the storm raging inside.

That night, I did not walk free. I was taken to central booking, fingerprinted, photographed, processed, and placed into a crowded holding cell where the hours felt eternal. The stench of sweat, the clang of metal bars, and the hum of despair pressed down on me. I prayed silently through the night, eyes fixed on nothing, ears tuned to every sound.

By morning, I stood before a judge. Bail was set, and only then was I allowed to step back into the daylight. Physically free, spiritually tethered, I whispered to myself:

*"The LORD is near to the brokenhearted and saves the crushed in spirit."* (Psalm 34:18)

# Second Arrest – The Weight of Repetition

Weeks later, the second arrest came, like a lightning strike I had anticipated but still dreaded. Zuleika had once again claimed I violated the order of protection. I had not spoken to her in any form. Yet, the machinery of the legal system pressed down with relentless weight.

Subpoenas for phone records, emails, and documentation piled up. Every knock, siren, and flashing light reminded me that my existence was being scrutinized. Even living at a relative's home—surrounded by familiarity—felt impermanent, like camping on borrowed time.

Prayer became my anchor:

- *"We are hard pressed on every side, but not crushed."* (2 Corinthians 4:8)
- *"No weapon formed against you shall prosper."* (Isaiah 54:17)

## Third Arrest – The Bishop Trap

By the third arrest, Zuleika had joined another ministry. The Bishop from that church reached out, requesting a meeting. I went in good faith, seeking resolution and trusting Scripture:

*"Dare any of you, having a matter against another, go to law before the unjust, and not before the saints?"* (1 Corinthians 6:1 KJV)

What I thought would be a reasonable and honorable conversation became a trap. My own Bishop, who had once appointed me as a minister, refused to help and instead sided with Zuleika. Later, he testified that my meeting violated the order of protection.

I had evidence of his prior misconduct with young parishioners—evidence that should have discredited him—but my attorney chose not to pursue it. I felt exposed and betrayed. What I thought was a step toward resolution became another legal and spiritual assault.

# Fourth Arrest – The Test of Endurance

The fourth arrest arrived under the cumulative weight of prior arrests. The DA sought more time—not because of new evidence but to let procedural momentum grind me down. Each police visit, each court appearance, each extension of the order of protection felt like punishment for simply existing.

Even without contacting Zuleika, I was dragged repeatedly into courts and stations. Each arrest deepened fear, and each delay tested patience, resilience, and faith.

I clung to Scripture:

- *"The righteous cry out, and the LORD hears them; he delivers them from all their troubles."* (Psalm 34:17)
- *"We are hard pressed on every side, but not crushed."* (2 Corinthians 4:8)

Through all this, I discovered a deeper truth: my identity is in Christ, unshaken by human systems, unjust judges, or betrayal from spiritual authorities.

## Daily Life Between Arrests

Life between arrests was a continuous balancing act. I lived at relatives' homes, surrounded by comfort but constantly reminded of impermanence. Every knock, every siren, every phone call felt like potential danger. Even ordinary daily tasks required vigilance to avoid any perception of violating the order of protection.

Emotionally, the strain was relentless. Fear, frustration, and exhaustion layered upon one another. I constantly replayed prior court appearances, interactions, and conversations, preparing for the next legal confrontation. Sleep was elusive; my mind remained alert, scanning for potential threats, replays of prior trauma, and possible traps.

Financially, the burden was crushing. Lawyers, court fees, and unexpected expenses drained my resources. Work became difficult; missed days due to court appearances or stress were unavoidable. Even when present at work, my mind was often elsewhere, rehearsing for the next legal challenge.

Spiritually, betrayal cut deepest. The Bishop who appointed me as a minister refused to protect me, siding with Zuleika. My attorney, rather than using the evidence I provided, chose not to act. I felt set up, trapped, and abandoned.

Yet, through these trials, I leaned on prayer and Scripture:

- *"The LORD will fight for you; you need only to be still."* (Exodus 14:14)
- *"No weapon formed against you shall prosper."* (Isaiah 54:17)
- *"I can do all things through Christ who strengthens me."* (Philippians 4:13)

## The Poison Episodes: Divine Protection

The danger wasn't just legal—it was physical. Zuleika had prepared food with malicious intent. The Holy Spirit warned me not to eat. Neither she nor her daughter touched the meals.

On one occasion, when she was distracted by her phone, I smeared a little food around my lips and quietly disposed of the rest in the garbage chute. On another, her daughter discreetly warned me not to eat, her eyes filled with quiet urgency.

Psalm 23:5 whispered in my spirit:

*"Thou preparest a table before me in the presence of mine enemies."*

Even in the midst of plots to destroy me, God's protection surrounded me. I hummed my song again, letting it rise in my chest:

*"…There is power in the name of Jesus, to break every chain…"*

## The Helpless Witness

The most agonizing moments were witnessing her daughter's abuse. On a school morning, I saw blood running from her nose, knowing I could not intervene. ACS was involved, and I confessed to both them and her school counselor. They asked if I needed help taking her to a safe space, but I refused, fearing retaliation.

It was heartbreaking that they later refused to testify about my confessions. My heart broke, yet God sustained me. At the onset of the abuse, I experienced palpitations, anxiety, and panic attacks. My primary care physician documented everything meticulously, providing notes that later became crucial. He referred me to a psychiatrist who began treatment immediately, also producing detailed reports.

Psalm 91:11 reminded me:

*"For He shall give His angels charge over thee, to keep thee in all thy ways."*

## Isolation in Church

Even in church, betrayal cut deep. One associate pastor admitted, "I do not know why the devil put it in my heart to hate you so much." Each time I shared updates, Zuleika somehow repeated my words verbatim, though no longer a member. I began to suspect the pastor's involvement.

There were moments of fear so extreme that He, the associate pastor surrendered his firearm, confessing violent thoughts. The threat was chilling.

Psalm 37:12–13 became real:

*"The wicked plotteth against the just, and gnasheth upon him with his teeth. The Lord shall laugh at him: for He seeth that his day is coming."*

Even then, I sang quietly:

*"…There is power in the name of Jesus, to break every chain…"*

## Beacons of Support

Two elder sisters stood unwaveringly by me, providing both financial and emotional support. One has since passed—may her soul rest in peace—but through their faith, I was reminded of God's remnant. These were beacons in the storm, reminding me that even when the world turned away, God preserved a faithful few.

## Financial and Emotional Exhaustion

Paying for multiple court cases drained me. Exhaustion threatened to end my fight. But Psalm 34:17–18 reminded me that God was near: *"The righteous cry, and the Lord heareth… The Lord is nigh unto them that are of a broken heart; and saveth such as be of a contrite spirit."*

I hummed and later sang my battle anthem aloud:

*"…There is power in the name of Jesus, to break every chain…"*

## Spiritual Armor and Inner Life

Panic attacks, anxiety, and fear were constant companions. Yet God provided strength through song, Scripture, and prayer. My cries to God were honest:

"Lord, why me? Protect my children, my name, my life."

Isaiah 41:10 whispered in my spirit:

*"Fear thou not; for I am with thee… I will uphold thee with the right hand of my righteousness."*

## Lessons in the Binding

- Weakness is the doorway to God's strength (2 Corinthians 12:9).
- Lies cannot erase God-given identity.
- Survival is a testimony of God's faithfulness.

## Prophetic Declaration

I declare in the name of Jesus: Though I have been bound, I will not be broken. No weapon formed against me shall prosper (Isaiah 54:17). Every tongue speaking falsely will be silenced. Every attempt to destroy me has been nullified by the power of Jesus.

I am pressed, but not crushed.

I am persecuted, but not abandoned.

I am struck down, but not destroyed.

I am bound, but not broken.

Psalm 91 and 2 Corinthians 4:8–9 breathe life into my testimony. Like Joseph, Daniel, and Paul, I stand, refined by fire, fully preserved by God's hand.

## A Glimpse of Victory

Even as frustration mounted, a quiet assurance whispered: justice would eventually break through the delay.

One morning, a small but significant victory came. The judge, recognizing that the ADA was simply letting the clock run without presenting any evidence, rebuked him publicly and ordered the proceedings to move forward.

To anyone else, it might have seemed minor, but to me, it was confirmation: God was orchestrating the outcome. The ADA's attempts to delay were no longer tolerated, and the system, for a brief moment, aligned with justice.

I stepped out of the courtroom, exhausted but strengthened.

Psalm 37:5 whispered in my spirit:

*"Commit thy way unto the Lord; trust also in him; and he shall bring it to pass."*

I hummed my battle anthem, louder this time, with renewed conviction:

*"…There is power in the name of Jesus, to break every chain…"*

Though the larger battles were far from over, this moment reminded me that God was actively intervening. Even the smallest sign of vindication reinforced that my faith was not in vain, and that every chain pressed against me was being transformed into strength.

## Transition to Chapter 9

But the fire was not finished refining me. Each courtroom victory seemed to trigger another attack, each moment of relief followed by a heavier blow. What I thought would end quickly only dragged on, exposing deeper betrayals, heavier accusations, and more painful isolation. Chapter 9 would open the door to an even darker valley—one where the furnace of affliction burned hotter, yet God's sustaining hand grew clearer.

# Chapter 9 – The God Who Sees

"You are the God who sees me." (Genesis 16:13)

## Zuleika's Mockery and the Weight of Fear

Zuleika was rejoicing, claiming victory as if every court order, every police visit, and every legal delay was divine confirmation that God was on her side. She walked with the confidence of someone who believed her lies had sealed my fate. To her, every summons was another trophy, another nail in the coffin of my reputation. Her laughter was cruel—it echoed like a weapon, slicing through my already weakened spirit.

Her celebration was more than arrogance—it was mockery, a brazen performance meant to convince others that she was righteous while I was condemned. She played the part of a saint while orchestrating chaos behind the curtain.

But I knew the truth: the devil is a liar. His voice may roar through human mouths, but it cannot silence the voice of God.

Still, her mockery seeped deep into me. My chest constricted until I could barely draw breath. My hands trembled so violently that it was difficult to hold a pen. My vision blurred with panic, and my heartbeat pounded so loud I thought others could hear it.

Fear, anger, frustration, and despair collided inside me like a storm breaking against rocks. Every knock on the door felt like a sentence. Every siren in the distance made me flinch. Every unopened envelope on the table felt like a time bomb.

In the quiet hours before dawn, when shadows stretched long and silence pressed in, anxiety crept into my bed like an intruder. The stillness was not comforting—it magnified the pounding of my heart. I walked the floorboards, back and forth, whispering fragments of Scripture like a soldier loading weapons in the dark.

*"God is our refuge and strength, a very present help in trouble."* (Psalm 46:1)

I repeated it until the words felt carved into the walls of my heart. Though the enemy pressed from every side, I was not without armor.

## The Workplace Ordeal

The afternoon the police came to my job, I felt their presence before I even saw them. There's a weight that precedes them— boots striking the tile, radios crackling, conversations suddenly hushed. My chest burned before they spoke a word. Sweat dampened the collar of my shirt. My knees weakened, and tears gathered against my will.

When they stepped into view, the lights above reflected off their badges. The gleam felt like a spotlight exposing me to the whole office. They carried papers in hand—the latest weapon Zuleika had forged against me: another order of protection.

The first time she sent officers to my workplace had been humiliating. Co-workers looked on with curiosity, their eyes full of silent questions. It was as though my private world had been dragged onto stage for public ridicule. I feared that every trip the police made into that building was another strike against my employment. I knew how fragile a reputation could be in professional spaces.

When they asked for me, someone pointed upstairs. My stomach dropped. Heat flooded my face as if the walls themselves accused me.

I forced myself to walk toward them. My legs felt like stone, my throat dry, but I said firmly, "I am not going to take this order of protection from you."

They exchanged looks, one raising an eyebrow. "What should we tell our boss?"

I swallowed hard, trembling, and replied, "I don't care."

I wanted someone—anyone—to stand beside me, but the HR administrator stepped in, taking the papers herself. I stood there, abandoned and exposed, disappointment stinging sharper than the officers' presence.

Each piece of paper Zuleika filed was crafted with malice. She knew the system well enough to twist it against me. A few days after filing, she would claim I violated it, and without question, the police would arrive to arrest me.

The air in the office thickened with gossip and suspicion. Even friendly conversations became cautious. Every glance felt weighted with unspoken judgment. I walked the halls like a marked man, my future dangling by a thread.

I clung to Psalm 37:5 like oxygen: *"Commit thy way unto the LORD; trust also in him; and he shall bring it to pass."*

## Traffic, Timing, and Court Appearances

Zuleika made another allegation that I had violated the order of protection yet another time. I was told to surrender myself after work. Even the road seemed to conspire against me. The highway crawled at a snail's pace. Brake lights stretched endlessly before me, glowing like warnings.

I kept glancing at the clock on the dash, as if time mattered anymore. They said to be there by seven. "Voluntary surrender," they'd called it — as if I had a choice. As if walking into a police station made me guilty by default.

I wasn't a criminal.

But somewhere in a system that no longer asked questions, only assigned labels, I had been stamped as one.

They said I violated the order — a piece of paper that could split lives with a single signature. One text, they claimed. One message, sent in a moment of confusion or desperation, and now I was the one under threat.

My lawyer told me to stay calm.

*"It'll sort itself out in court. Just follow the process."*

But the process didn't see me. It didn't see the context, the history, the truth behind a misstep. It just saw a name on a docket, a box checked, and a cell waiting.

My hands gripped the wheel so tightly the leather cut into my palms. Sweat rolled down my temples. Every honk felt like an accusation. My stomach twisted violently, and my chest tightened until each breath came shallow. I dialed my attorney again and again: "I'm running late. She knows I'm on the way."

Every red light felt like judgment. Every green light felt too short. I whispered Scripture at each stop, trying to drown out the rising panic:

*"For He shall give His angels charge over thee, to keep thee in all thy ways."* (Psalm 91:11)

Even in traffic, I saw the unseen hand of God. Though my body trembled and my vision blurred, I knew He was arranging the details. Each delay, each turn, each mile was part of His orchestration.

# Arrests and Divine Timing

The system tested me over and over, grinding me down with repetition. Yet, in every arrest, I could trace the fingerprints of God's timing.

- **The Saturday Arrest:** I was taken in late at night, handcuffed under harsh fluorescent lights, my dignity stripped by the echo of cell doors slamming shut. I spent the night in central booking, surrounded by the restless breathing and muffled curses of strangers. The cement was cold against my back. The stench of sweat and fear hung thick in the air. Sleep was impossible. In the morning, bleary-eyed and hollow, I stood before the judge. Bail was granted. Hours later, I was back behind the pulpit, preaching. My hands still shook, my body still weak, but peace wrapped me like a cloak. That sermon was not strength—it was survival.
- **The Friday Surrender:** Another time, I was allowed to finish my workweek before turning myself in. Traffic nearly destroyed the plan. My attorney and I stayed in constant contact, every message a lifeline. My chest clenched with panic as the minutes ticked down, but I arrived—just in time. That night, I whispered thanks, knowing even the timing of traffic lights was in God's control.

Psalm 34:17–18 steadied me: *"The righteous cry, and the LORD heareth, and delivereth them out of all their troubles. The LORD is nigh unto them that are of a broken heart."*

## Physical and Emotional Strain

The pressure hollowed me out. Sleep became a distant memory. My body felt like it was running on fumes. Meals were skipped, water forgotten, my strength slipping away.

Panic attacks stalked me like predators. My chest tightened until I gasped for air. My hands shook uncontrollably. My vision narrowed until the world blurred. It felt as though my own body was betraying me.

But I turned even panic into prayer. My battle anthem rose from my lips like a shield:

*"...There is power in the name of Jesus, to break every chain..."*

Each time the fear threatened to swallow me, I sang it louder, until the tremors in my body aligned with the rhythm of faith.

Isaiah 41:10 became my whispered defiance: *"Fear thou not; for I am with thee... I will uphold thee with the right hand of my righteousness."*

## Family Support and Confrontation

My aunt, with whom I lived, became a fortress in human form. She carried me when I was too weak, offered her home when I had none, and defended me when I was too weary to speak.

One Sunday, after church, Zuleika confronted her. She slipped off her shoes just outside the church building, ready to brawl because my aunt had rebuked her for publicly disrespecting me. Her eyes blazed with rage, her posture coiled for violence.

But my aunt did not flinch. She stood firmly, her presence unshaken. God's Spirit surrounded her like a shield. The confrontation did not explode because God Himself stepped between us.

Even in moments like that, I saw His timing—how He allowed just enough to be revealed but prevented destruction.

## Shifting Emotions and Spiritual Anchoring

My emotions swung like a pendulum. Some days, fear gripped me so tightly it stole my breath. Other days, anger surged like fire, demanding release. At times, despair pressed so heavily that I could barely lift my head. But then came moments of peace— unexpected, divine, unexplainable.

I began to notice the small fingerprints of God in places others might dismiss:

- A judge raises an eyebrow at the ADA's baseless claims.
- A delay that seemed harmful but ultimately revealed lies.
- A forgotten document surfacing at just the right time.

Psalm 37:23–24 reminded me daily: *"The steps of a good man are ordered by the LORD… Though he fall, he shall not be utterly cast down: for the LORD upholdeth him with his hand."*

I started journaling each intervention. Each entry became a stone of remembrance, proof that God was not silent even when the storm roared.

## Persistent Fear and Faith

My greatest fear was prison. I knew the statistics. I knew the history of innocent Black men swallowed by the system, condemned for crimes they never committed. Every hearing carried that possibility. The thought alone was suffocating.

But even when fear pressed against me, faith pressed back harder. I repeated my verses, hummed my anthem, and prayed through clenched teeth.

Psalm 91:1–2 became my dwelling place: *"He that dwelleth in the secret place of the most High shall abide under the shadow of the*

*Almighty. I will say of the LORD, He is my refuge and my fortress: my God; in him will I trust."*

## Witnessing Evil, Remaining Faithful

The hardest blows were not against me—they were the moments I saw Zuleika's manipulation at work or glimpsed the signs of her daughter's abuse. To see lies paraded as truth, to watch an innocent child suffer, and to feel powerless—that was a wound deeper than any courtroom.

I documented what I could. I reported what I could. And then I prayed, trusting the God who sees.

Psalm 23:5 comforted me: *"Thou preparest a table before me in the presence of mine enemies."*

Though I could not stop every injustice, I held fast to the God who sees all.

## Prophetic Declaration

I declare in the name of Jesus:

- You, Lord, see every injustice, every lie, every attempt to destroy me.
- I am pressed, but not crushed.
- I am persecuted, but not abandoned.
- I am struck down, but not destroyed.
- I am bound, but not broken.

Psalm 91 and 2 Corinthians 4:8–9 breathe life into my testimony. Like Joseph in prison, Daniel in the lions' den, and Paul in chains, I stand—not defeated, but preserved by the God who sees.

# A Glimpse of Victory

Even in the bleakest moments, God whispered hope.

One morning, in a crowded courtroom buzzing with voices and echoing footsteps, the judge's patience finally snapped. He turned on the ADA, rebuking him for stalling without presenting evidence. His words cracked through the room like thunder: "This case must move forward."

To anyone else, it may have seemed minor. To me, it was a glimpse of divine justice.

As I stepped out of the courthouse, the city's noise felt lighter. My legs were weak, but my spirit steadied. Psalm 37:5 whispered again: *"Commit thy way unto the LORD; trust also in him; and he shall bring it to pass."*

I hummed my anthem, louder this time, my voice mingling with the rush of traffic and the chatter of strangers:

*"...There is power in the name of Jesus, to break every chain..."*

Though the war was far from over, I knew God had seen me. And if He had seen me here, He would see me through the next storm.

# Chapter 10 – Breaking Covenant, Finding Freedom

"Dare any of you, having a matter against another, go to law before the unjust, and not before the saints?" (1 Corinthians 6:1)

*Sometimes, freedom comes only after we are forced to confront what has bound us. This chapter explores the moment of release, the divine wisdom that protects us, and the grief that accompanies the breaking of chains.*

## The Breaking Point

By the time she had me arrested the second time, something inside me snapped. It wasn't just anger or frustration—it was the moment of clarity when I finally realized that no matter how much I prayed, no matter how much I sacrificed, no matter how much I tried to "make it work," Zuleika had no desire for reconciliation.

She wasn't interested in peace. She wasn't interested in healing. She was interested only in control.

I had hoped, even pleaded with God at times, that things might change. But as the days turned into weeks, it became undeniable: she had no intention of salvaging the marriage. What she wanted was to dominate, to manipulate, to bend me to her will.

That day, I made a decision. Her control had to be broken. I would not let my life, my freedom, my very soul be consumed any longer. I decided to proceed with the divorce—not out of bitterness, but out of necessity for survival.

**Ecclesiastes 3:6**

"A time to keep, and a time to cast away."

I had kept the covenant as long as I could, but now it was time to cast away the chains that had been strangling my spirit.

## Serving the Papers

Filing the case was one thing; serving her was another. I hired professional process servers who came prepared for exactly the kind of confrontation they suspected they would face. These were not men who wandered casually into the job—they had experience, and they came ready. They carried cameras, documentation, and her photograph to ensure there was no mistake.

When they arrived, they called out her name. Boldly. Publicly. "Zuleika."

She responded. She acknowledged who she was. At that moment, the servers placed the documents in her hands and officially served her.

This was no mistake, no trick, no confusion. It was recorded, documented, and undeniable.

It was strangely symbolic—she who had tried so hard to trap me was now caught by her own name, her own answer.

**Proverbs 26:27**

"Whoever digs a pit will fall into it, and he who rolls a stone will have it roll back on him."

# Fast-Tracked Proceedings

The divorce process itself was shockingly quick. Because she failed to respond to the summons, the case moved forward uncontested. What could have dragged on for years was resolved in just about three months.

When the decree was finalized, I felt the weight of months—years, really—begin to lift.

But Zuleika was not done. She filed an appeal, claiming she had never been served. She said the divorce was "illegally obtained," even though the process servers had filed a meticulous report. Her lies were unraveling, but she still fought to weave another web.

In her appeal, she demanded things that revealed her true motives:

- The BMW—claiming she had purchased it, though she had no means of affording it.
- Alimony—though we had only been married just over four months.

When her demands reached the courtroom, the judge did not entertain them. My attorney submitted the process servers' documentation to her attorney, to the criminal court judge, and to the family court judge. Every angle was covered. The truth spoke louder than her lies.

The judge told her plainly: she would not be receiving alimony. The marriage had ended almost as soon as it began, and her claims held no weight.

**Proverbs 19:5**

"A false witness will not go unpunished, and he who breathes out lies will not escape."

# The Trap That Failed

It wasn't only about cars or money. Looking back, I remembered how quickly after we were married, she had pressed for a child. The urgency with which she pursued it puzzled me at first. I told her time and again, "I'm not ready. Mentally, I'm not there. We don't have the space. The timing isn't right."

At the time, I thought it was just an issue of wisdom or timing. But now I know—it was God Himself blocking that trap.

If I had given in, if I had fathered a child with Zuleika, she would have used that child as a permanent chain. She would have ensured I paid child support to the maximum, binding me to her manipulation for life.

**Psalm 139:1–2**

"O Lord, You have searched me and known me. You know my sitting down and my rising up; You understand my thought afar off."

God saw my future before I did. He knew the devastation that would have unfolded if I had gone down that path. It was His Spirit that gave me the wisdom to say no. It was His mercy that prevented a seed from being planted, that stopped a chain before it could even form.

# The Moment of Release

When the gavel struck and the divorce was finalized, the sound reverberated deep within me. It wasn't just the end of a marriage; it was the breaking of a yoke.

I grieved deeply that day. It felt like burying a dream, a covenant, a promise I had once made before God and man. Yet alongside the grief was a strange sense of freedom.

I realized that day that freedom often comes with tears. It doesn't always feel like victory in the moment—it feels like loss. But in the Kingdom of God, loss can be the doorway to life.

**John 12:24**

"Unless a grain of wheat falls into the earth and dies, it remains alone; but if it dies, it bears much fruit."

Walking out of the courtroom, I wasn't jubilant or triumphant. I was sober, reflective, but steady. For the first time in a long time, I was free.

## God's Presence in the Breaking

In the aftermath, I wrestled with the hard questions. "Did I fail? Did I let God down by divorcing?"

Each time, His Word reassured me. Malachi 2:16 was often used as a weapon against me: "God hates divorce." But when I looked deeper, I saw that the same Scripture also says God hates violence and treachery in marriage. How could I dishonor God more—by staying chained to abuse, or by stepping into the freedom He provided?

**Hebrews 13:5**

"I will never leave you nor forsake you."

Even in my darkest valley, even in the courthouse, God had been with me. I began to see that His hand had guided me at every step:

- Protecting me from being ensnared by traps I could not foresee.
- Shielding me from financial ruin when her claims were denied.
- Covering me when false accusations rose up again and again.
- Delivering me when the court system could not.

The divorce was not the end of me—it was the end of her control over me. It was the doorway into freedom.

**Isaiah 43:18–19**

"Do not remember the former things, nor consider the things of old. Behold, I will do a new thing; now it shall spring forth; shall you not know it? I will even make a road in the wilderness and rivers in the desert."

God was not finished with me. This was just the beginning of the release.

## Reflection Questions

1. How have you experienced freedom from a situation only to realize there was still pain to process?
2. What emotions are you holding back that need to be poured out before God?
3. In what ways can acknowledging grief help you step into true healing and restoration?
4. How can Scripture guide you in navigating the tension between freedom and sorrow?

## Prayer Starter

"Lord, I thank You for delivering me from what held me captive. But I also bring before You the grief, the sorrow, and the wounds that remain. Help me to pour out my heart honestly before You, to let the tears and prayers rise as a sweet offering. Teach me to trust that You are near, that You will restore what has been broken, and that Your promise of redemption is sure. Let me walk forward in freedom, yet never bypass the healing You provide. In Jesus' name, Amen."

## Transition to Chapter 11

Though the marriage covenant was now legally broken, the battle was far from over. Freedom had come at a cost, and while the weight of her control was lifted, the ripple effects of her accusations, lies, and manipulations still lingered in every corner of my life. The courts had not finished with me, the whispers in church had not silenced, and the wounds in my spirit were still raw. Yet in those fragile moments of release, I began to sense that God was preparing me for something greater. What the enemy had meant for destruction, the Lord was already reshaping into testimony. Chapter 11 would not be about chains or papers—it would be about the God who restores what has been stolen and gives new life where ashes once remained.

# Chapter 11 – Learning to Lament

"Pour out your heart like water before the Lord." — Lamentations 2:19

## Introduction

Lament is a spiritual discipline often misunderstood. Many equate tears with weakness or despair with failure, yet lament is a sacred act of honesty before God. In this chapter, I share how grief, worship, and prayer became the bridge to restoration in the aftermath of divorce and injustice.

## The Gym Encounter and the Weight of Injustice

There are certainly benefits to being married—companionship, shared vision, covenantal commitment. Yet, in the aftermath of my divorce, I realized I was not missing anything. Freedom came with a strange peace, knowing that Zuleika had no love for me and was on a path to destroy the life of someone else, should I remain entangled.

From that time forward, my life narrowed to home, work, and church. No social life. No distractions. I even canceled my gym membership after a Saturday that shook me to my core.

I had gone to the gym that morning as part of my routine. The air smelled faintly of disinfectant and rubber mats, the clink of weights echoing in the background. But on the way, I noticed Zuleika on the sidewalk. My heart sank into my stomach. I knew she was scheming. By the time I left the gym, heading back to my car, she emerged from a nearby store, phone in hand, snapping multiple photos of me.

She had laid in wait, anticipating my every move. Once she had her images, she called her attorney, claiming I was stalking her. Can you imagine? The one who had been harassing me, following me, waiting to fabricate an incident, now had the audacity to accuse me.

I called the police, hoping for justice. Their response was flat, almost indifferent: "There's nothing we can do. It's a public place." The words stung worse than silence. I tried to obtain an order of protection through the courts, but it was denied. Meanwhile, she secured an extension on her order of protection against me.

How unjust. How unfair.

It was a vivid demonstration of Habakkuk's warning:

"Therefore the law is slacked, and judgment doth never go forth: for the wicked doth compass about the righteous; therefore wrong judgment proceedeth." (Habakkuk 1:4)

This injustice became a shadow that followed me into every quiet moment. It was not merely an emotional weight—it was spiritual. I could not rely on human systems for protection. I had to bring my pain before God.

Even as I faced this injustice, I noticed the internal battle raging within me: frustration, anger, grief, and at times profound exhaustion that weighed on my soul like a physical force. I wrestled with questions: "Why is this happening? How long will this continue? Will God ever intervene?"

The questions echoed like footsteps in an empty hall. Every knock, every siren, every flicker of light on the street at night carried fresh anxiety. Even mundane routines became triggers, stirring reminders of Zuleika's manipulation and the fragile injustice of the system.

## Silence and Reflection

After the gym incident, silence enveloped me. The noise of courtrooms, lawyers, accusations, and gavel strikes was gone. In its place was a heavy, reflective quiet. My life had shrunk: home, work, church. The gym was gone, social outings canceled.

Silence forced me to face the aftermath fully, and that reflection was painful.

The psalmist wrote:

"He sitteth alone and keepeth silence, because he hath borne it upon him. He putteth his mouth in the dust; if so be there may be hope." (Lamentations 3:28–29)

This verse captured my reality. Silence was both suffocating and sacred. It was in that quiet that I began to understand that lament was necessary—not optional—for healing.

At night, I would hear the hum of the refrigerator or the tick of a clock, and the stillness pressed on me like a weight. In those silent hours, my mind replayed every accusation, every arrest, every humiliation. Regret tried to creep in, whispering "what if," but Scripture fought back, speaking hope into the void.

## The Physical and Emotional Weight of Lament

I experienced lament with my whole body. Some nights, I paced the floor until exhaustion claimed me. My footsteps sounded like thunder in my ears, though the room was still. Other nights, I sat on the floor, back against the wall, tears soaking into my shirt until my body finally gave out.

Sometimes, the crying gave me migraine headaches so fierce I had to lie down in the darkness. Other nights, my chest tightened, and I fought to breathe through shallow gasps.

My prayers were often silent. Groans rose from my chest that I could not put into words. Romans 8:26 was not a distant verse; it was my reality:

"Likewise, the Spirit also helpeth our infirmities: for we know not what we should pray for as we ought, but the Spirit itself maketh intercession for us with groanings which cannot be uttered."

Even when I couldn't find words, the Spirit carried my lament upward.

## Psalms as Sanctuary

When words failed, the Psalms gave me language. They became my prayers, my confessions, my comfort, my shield.

- **Psalm 13**: taught me to question God honestly in despair.
- **Psalm 42**: reminded me that hope still lives beneath turmoil.
- **Psalm 55**: gave me words for betrayal, teaching me to hand it over to God.

One night, I lay awake, eyes burning from tears, whispering Psalm 34:17–18 over and over until I fell asleep:

"The righteous cry, and the LORD heareth, and delivereth them out of all their troubles. The LORD is nigh unto them that are of a broken heart; and saveth such as be of a contrite spirit."

Those words became a balm. They weren't just read; they were breathed into my soul.

## Worship as Weapon

Even amid lament, worship became my weapon. One song, in particular, became my anthem:

"There is power in the name of Jesus to break every chain."

I sang it alone, sometimes quietly, sometimes loud, sometimes through tears so heavy my voice cracked.

Like Paul and Silas in the Philippian jail, I discovered that worship could rattle invisible chains even before the cell doors swung open (Acts 16:25–26). My "earthquake" wasn't external—it was in my spirit. After singing, I often felt a peace that settled on me like a blanket. Not dramatic, but undeniable.

## Wrestling with Pressure and Conceding

Friends, family, even people in the church suggested I should concede, move on, or simply "forgive and forget." But lament demanded honesty. And honesty required that I face the full depth of my pain before God.

Even Jesus, in Gethsemane, cried out in anguish, sweating drops of blood. My lament, then, was not failure—it was faith.

## The Pain and Temporary Relief

Nights of lament were brutal. Tears left me swollen-eyed and weak. Yet even in the exhaustion, I sensed God drawing near.

Sometimes the relief came in whispers—like waking up with enough strength to face the day, or sensing a Scripture rise up in my heart as armor against despair. Other times, it came through unexpected reminders of His presence—a text from a believer, a song on the radio, a moment of clarity I could not manufacture myself.

These were God's fingerprints. Small mercies, quiet confirmations.

## Hope Hidden in Lament

Gradually, lament shifted from despair to hope. Ashes began to show signs of beauty. I started noticing subtle signs of God's hand:

- A delay in court that worked in my favor.
- Strength on a day when I thought I couldn't go on.
- Clarity in prayer where confusion once lived.

Isaiah 61:3 came alive:

"To grant to them that mourn in Zion—to give them beauty for ashes, the oil of joy for mourning, the garment of praise for the spirit of heaviness."

The night was long, yes—but I began to believe Psalm 30:5:

"Weeping may endure for a night, but joy cometh in the morning."

## Reflections on the Discipline of Lament

Lament is not weakness. It is not defeat. It is worship in the wilderness. It is faith refusing to be silent before God in the face of suffering.

- It allows grief to surface rather than fester.
- It teaches us to bring our raw, honest selves before God.
- It trains our hearts to recognize His presence, even in pain.
- It transforms sorrow into seeds of hope.

As Lamentations 2:19 calls us:

"Pour out your heart like water before the Lord."

And so I did.

## Reflection Questions

1. Have you ever mistaken lament for weakness instead of worship?
2. What griefs are you holding back that God is inviting you to pour out?
3. How can Scripture guide you in processing pain instead of ignoring it?
4. Can you identify moments when tears, groans, or worship became spiritual weapons in your life?
5. Where have you glimpsed God's presence in the small, ordinary moments of your grief?

## Prayer Starter

"Lord, I come before You with my grief, my sorrow, my confusion, and my anger. I pour out my heart like water before You, trusting that You see me, that You hear me, and that You will transform this pain into strength, joy, and praise. Teach me to lament faithfully, to worship through tears, and to trust You even when I do not understand. In Jesus' name, Amen."

## Transition to Chapter 12

Lament was not the end of my journey—it was the doorway to healing. In the silence of tears, God was planting seeds of restoration. As I learned to bring my sorrow honestly before Him, I also began to notice something new stirring: hope.

The next chapter explores how God began to **rebuild my identity piece by piece**, showing me that the ashes of lament were not the conclusion, but the soil for resurrection.

# Chapter 12 – Redemption and Release

"Remember ye not the former things, neither consider the things of old.

Behold, I will do a new thing; now it shall spring forth; shall ye not know it?

I will even make a way in the wilderness, and rivers in the desert."

— Isaiah 43:18–19

## The Weight of Letting Go

Letting go was not easy. In fact, it felt impossible. The hardest thing to release was not just one emotion—it was *everything*: the regret of wasted years, the fear of what might come next, the anger at being falsely accused, and the deep desire for justice.

The judicial system made the weight even heavier. As a man falsely accused, there was no avenue to counter-sue or bring accountability. The system leaned to protect accusers, even when their credibility had been shredded. While this principle may protect women in real danger, men like me were left to suffer—emotionally, physically, and financially—with no remedy when the accusations proved false.

It was unfair. It was unjust. And yet God's Word met me even there:

"Brethren, I count not myself to have apprehended: but this one thing I do, forgetting those things which are behind, and reaching forth unto those things which are before,

I press toward the mark for the prize of the high calling of God in Christ Jesus." (Philippians 3:13–14)

Forgetting did not mean erasing. It meant refusing to let bitterness dictate the future. Letting go became an act of faith—a choice to believe that God Himself would bring justice, healing, and restoration in His way and in His time.

## The Daily Struggle and Spiritual Wrestling

The cases dragged on for more than two years. Each court date felt like another weight pressing on my chest. Zuleika, her attorneys, and the ADA seemed determined to wear me down, clinging to the faint hope that I would slip up.

Each morning, I woke with anxiety. Thoughts replayed over and over: *What if the judge believes her? What if this drags on forever?* My sleep was restless, filled with tension and nightmares of legal defeat.

Yet even in that fear, I turned to Scripture:

"The LORD is my light and my salvation; whom shall I fear?

The LORD is the strength of my life; of whom shall I be afraid?" (Psalm 27:1)

I wrestled internally. I questioned God, asking why this injustice had to continue. And yet, every day, I sensed His presence. I felt a quiet assurance that He had not abandoned me, that His justice would prevail in His timing.

## The Courtroom Battle: God's Justice Revealed

Finally, the day came. A new judge sat on the bench. Her demeanor was firm, decisive, and unshaken. She leaned forward, eyes sharp, tone clipped as she pressed the ADA for evidence. He had nothing—no facts, no proof, nothing but delay after delay.

The courtroom was tense. I could hear the scratch of pens, the shuffle of papers, the hum of the fluorescent lights above. My own breathing sounded loud in my ears. My lawyer sat beside me, lips pressed tight, waiting for the judge's words.

Then came the moment:

"We are not doing this… all four cases are dismissed. Mr. Cordell, you are free to go."

The words echoed in my soul like a bell ringing through the ages. My chest tightened, then released. Tears welled up, blurring the bench before me. I whispered, *"Thank You, Lord."* My attorney exhaled with relief. A faint murmur rippled through the courtroom—surprise, disbelief, but undeniable closure.

Years of false accusations, sleepless nights, financial strain, and emotional torment culminated in this single declaration of freedom.

"The righteous cry, and the LORD heareth, and delivereth them out of all their troubles.

The LORD is nigh unto them that are of a broken heart; and saveth such as be of a contrite spirit." (Psalm 34:17–18)

At that moment, I realized God's justice is not always immediate, but it is sure. Every tear, every prayer, every moment of waiting had been acknowledged.

## Forgiveness: Praying for the Unrepentant

Even as my vindication unfolded, forgiveness played a crucial role. I prayed that the Lord would truly save Zuleika. She felt justified in her wrongs, and only God could see her heart. But I hoped for her repentance.

"Then said Jesus, Father, forgive them; for they know not what they do." (Luke 23:34)

"Lord, lay not this sin to their charge." (Acts 7:60)

Forgiveness did not excuse her actions. It allowed me to release her to God, freeing me from bitterness and rage, and enabling me to embrace peace. Peace became a deliberate choice, not a passive feeling.

## Observing God's Hand in Small Victories

Even as the legal saga continued, I began to notice subtle signs of redemption:

- Peace abiding in me, even amid chaos.
- Joy slowly returning, replacing heaviness.
- New friendships forming, providing encouragement.
- No desire to rush into dating, focusing on healing first.

Meanwhile, Zuleika's life was unraveling. Her ten-year struggle to complete an Associate's Degree revealed her academic inability, laziness, and attempts to coerce others into doing her work. Financially, she faced lawsuits, defaulted rent, and eviction. God's justice was quietly at work.

"Be not deceived; God is not mocked: for whatsoever a man soweth, that shall he also reap." (Galatians 6:7)

"But as for you, ye thought evil against me; but God meant it unto good, to bring to pass, as it is this day, to save much people alive." (Genesis 50:20)

The irony was clear: while her schemes fell apart, God was piecing me back together.

## Identity Shift: From Victim to Beloved

Before release, I felt broken, forgotten, and victimized. After the dismissal, everything shifted.

"In whom we have redemption through his blood, the forgiveness of sins, according to the riches of his grace." (Ephesians 1:7)

I began to see myself as God sees me: redeemed, beloved, purposeful. My scars were not marks of defeat but testaments to His grace. I was no longer "the accused." I was "the redeemed."

## Walking in Freedom

Release was not a one-time courtroom victory—it became a daily practice:

- Prayer and worship anchored my spirit.
- Scripture saturated my mind with truth.
- Friendships provided community and accountability.
- When old memories resurfaced, I consciously chose to resist, declaring: *"I am free."*

"If the Son therefore shall make you free, ye shall be free indeed." (John 8:36)

Freedom was tangible—it was in spirit, mind, and actions. It was not the absence of memories, but the presence of peace.

## Reflections on Redemption and Release

- Redemption is God's work. My part was surrender.
- Release is strength, not weakness. It takes courage to trust God's justice over our own.
- Freedom is forward-facing. My past was real, but it no longer ruled me.
- Scars are testimonies of grace. They demonstrate God's sustaining power.
- Victory is God's glory. Every tear, sleepless night, and moment of waiting refined and strengthened me.

## Looking Back: Growth and Transformation

Reflecting on the entire journey, I realized the transformation was profound:

- The boy who felt powerless and victimized became a man rooted in faith.
- Daily struggles forged endurance.
- Worship, prayer, and Scripture practice became armor.
- The enemy's schemes, intended for evil, revealed God's power for good.

The stage was now set for the next chapter: walking forward with strength, purpose, and unwavering faith.

## Reflection Questions

1. What burdens—anger, regret, desire for control—are you still holding that God is calling you to release?
2. How have you seen God's fingerprints in small new beginnings?
3. How does forgiveness—whether instant or gradual—play into your own release?

4. What Scriptures speak most to your identity in Christ rather than your past?
5. What daily practices could help you remain in freedom instead of rehearsing the pain?
6. How does Joseph's or Job's story mirror your own experience of waiting, suffering, and vindication?
7. Where have you noticed subtle victories that reflect God's hand even in prolonged struggles?

## Prayer Starter

"Lord, I release to You the regret, fear, anger, and desire for justice that I cannot carry. I surrender every weight to Your hands, trusting You to redeem what was broken and to restore what was lost. Thank You for calling me beloved, for rewriting my story, and for giving me peace that passes understanding. Help me to walk daily in freedom, to forgive as I have been forgiven, and to trust that what the enemy meant for evil, You have turned for good. In Jesus' name, Amen."

## Transition into Chapter 13

Though the gavel had fallen, declaring my release, my story was far from over. Freedom was not simply about being cleared in a courtroom—it was about learning to live again, to trust again, to dream again. The Lord had broken the chains of accusation, but He was also calling me to step into a greater purpose.

# Chapter 13 – The Strength to Stand

*"I can do all things through Christ which strengtheneth me."*

— Philippians 4:13

## Rebuilding from the Ground Up

After the long battle with Zuleika—the arrests, the endless court cases, the false accusations—the challenge ahead was clear: I had to rebuild my life from the ground up.

Every area had been shaken—trust, self-confidence, friendships, even my career. Decisions that once came easily now carried a weight. Could I trust a friend with my thoughts? Could I invest in my career without the fear of sabotage? Could I open my heart again without risking the same destruction?

Some mornings, the struggle started before I even opened my eyes. My chest felt heavy, as though yesterday's burdens had crept into the new day. I whispered prayers while still in bed:

*"Lord, give me strength today. Help me not to carry yesterday's pain."*

Over time, I learned that strength didn't come all at once. Sometimes it came in small victories: a full night's sleep without nightmares, a sunrise watched quietly on the balcony while sipping coffee, the stillness reminding me that God's peace was slowly seeping back in.

Even ordinary routines became spiritual exercises. Commuting to work in traffic, I would grip the steering wheel, silently narrating my worries to God, asking Him to guide each step. Walking into the office, I breathed prayers under my breath: *"Cover me, Lord.*

*Guard my mind."* These small, consistent acts of trust were the bricks and mortar of my rebuilding.

## Friendships and Community

Though much of my healing happened in solitude, strength also came through friendships. Trusted friends became lifelines.

I remember sitting in a café one afternoon with a close friend. The smell of roasted coffee filled the air as I quietly confessed how drained I felt, how the accusations still haunted me. He leaned forward, looked me straight in the eyes, and said, *"You're stronger than you know. God has already carried you through the worst."* Those words settled deep in my spirit, like water poured on dry ground.

Others sent me Scriptures at the exact moments I needed them:

- *"Fear thou not; for I am with thee: be not dismayed; for I am thy God."* (Isaiah 41:10)
- *"The LORD is my light and my salvation; whom shall I fear?"* (Psalm 27:1)

Even short texts or brief phone calls felt like reminders that I wasn't forgotten. I also found myself reaching out to encourage others, realizing that when I shared Scripture with someone else, my own spirit was lifted. Community became a mirror of God's presence—His way of reminding me that I was never alone.

## Ministry and Pastoral Encounter

Eventually, I moved away from my former church, seeking clarity and distance. My relationship with the pastor was cautiously restored, and one day he approached me about taking over a ministry he believed I had left unfinished.

At first, I felt curiosity—maybe this was an opportunity to serve again. But hesitation lingered. Could I trust someone who had mishandled my pain?

I told him I would only consider it if he first spoke with my current leader and received his blessing. When the conversation happened, I was present, listening as he recounted every detail of my ordeal with Zuleika. Hearing it all over again felt like reopening a wound that had barely healed. The room seemed colder, my chest tightened, and I realized with startling clarity: I had no desire to return to his ministry.

I forgave him, recognizing that age and human weakness may have clouded his judgment. But I also learned an important truth— **forgiveness does not require resuming a relationship.** Boundaries are not unspiritual; they are essential for protection, for peace, and for guarding the call of God on one's life.

## The Appellate Court Challenge

Even after the initial courtroom victories, Zuleika was not finished.

One gray morning, I sat in the family court waiting room, fluorescent lights buzzing above, the weight of dread heavy on my chest. Her attorney filed yet another appeal. When we entered the courtroom, the judge sighed with visible frustration.

"What relief are you seeking this time?" she asked sharply.

Her attorney requested punitive measures. To avoid months of prolonged conflict, I agreed to a six-month order of protection. It was a compromise, but one that spared me more endless hearings.

As we left the courtroom, Zuleika proudly lifted her chin and declared, *"Thank you, Jesus. Victory is mine."*

Her words stung, but deep inside, I knew the truth: **victory does not come from gloating in court. Victory comes from Christ.** As I walked to my car, the cool air brushing against my face, I whispered, *"Lord, You are my true vindication. I will not be shaken by false celebrations."*

That day, I realized something profound—she was still chasing courtroom wins, while I was walking in eternal peace.

## Emotional and Physical Tension

Every court appearance exacted a physical toll. My throat would tighten, my palms would sweat, and my chest would ache as I listened to lawyers argue. At times, I found myself gripping the wooden edge of the courtroom pew, whispering prayers between clenched teeth:

*"Be still, and know that I am God."* (Psalm 46:10)

*"The LORD is my rock, and my fortress, and my deliverer."* (Psalm 18:2)

Though fear threatened to consume me, peace would often descend like a gentle blanket. It wasn't dramatic, but it was enough to steady my breathing and remind me that God was present even there.

## Spiritual Disciplines

During this season, my survival depended on spiritual discipline. Prayer became my lifeline. Worship became my weapon. Bible study grounded me in truth when lies swirled around me. Journaling helped me trace God's fingerprints, even on days when they seemed invisible.

One evening, after a long day in court, I sat in my living room with my Bible open and journal nearby. As I wrote, I realized that small acts—praying before meals, humming worship songs while cooking, meditating on Scripture while walking—were stitching me back together. They were like threads of light weaving through my darkest nights.

## Embracing Identity and Purpose

The enemy had intended to crush me, but God had used the trial to rebuild me. Confidence returned, slowly but surely. I found freedom in decision-making, resilience in setbacks, and even joy in simple things like walking through the park at dusk or watching the horizon melt into shades of orange and purple.

I intentionally delayed dating, choosing instead to focus on healing. My heart needed time to be restored, and I trusted that God would guide me when the time was right.

Every quiet moment of reflection reminded me: **I was not just surviving anymore. I was living again.**

## Biblical Parallels

As I rebuilt, I found myself drawn to the stories of Joseph, Job, David, and Paul. Each had endured betrayal, loss, or false accusation, yet each emerged stronger, rooted in faith. Their stories echoed my own, reminding me that suffering is never wasted in God's hands.

Joseph's vindication after betrayal, Job's restoration after suffering, David's psalms of lament, and Paul's endurance through persecution—each story became a mirror and a mentor for my own.

## Daily Reflections

I began to notice God in the smallest details:

- Morning coffee paired with whispered gratitude.
- Running errands while praying under my breath.
- Encouraging a friend with a simple text.
- Journaling at night, listing both struggles and victories.

Every small moment became proof that life after devastation was not only possible but purposeful.

## Transition to Chapter 14

As strength returned, I began to sense something stirring—purpose. God had not simply brought me through the fire so I could rebuild a quiet, private life. He had preserved me for something greater.

The trials were not wasted. The pain was not meaningless. Everything I endured was preparing me for a higher calling.

The next chapter of my journey would not be about surviving or even rebuilding—it would be about stepping into purpose, walking boldly into the future God had ordained for me.

# Chapter 14 – Beauty for Ashes

*"To grant to them that mourn in Zion—to give them beauty for ashes, the oil of joy for mourning, the garment of praise for the spirit of heaviness; that they may be called trees of righteousness, the planting of the Lord, that He may be glorified."*

— Isaiah 61:3

## From Ashes to Renewal

After years of fire—false accusations, humiliating arrests, and courtrooms where my life was treated like a spectacle—I stepped into a season that felt like a sunrise after a long night.

The ashes were real. I carried the memories of betrayal, the regret of wasted time, the heaviness of scars no one else could see. But God was faithful to His promise. Out of those ashes, He began to create something beautiful: a new chapter, filled not with fear but with peace.

That peace came when I met my wife. From the beginning, she carried herself with grace. She never once judged me for what I had endured. She never weaponized my past or brought it up to shame me. Instead, she looked at me with eyes that saw beyond the scars to the man God had refined in the fire.

I knew I was healed when I could tell my story without bitterness—when I could look back at the wreckage and not feel anger rise up inside me. My scars became like trophies of survival, visible reminders that God restores what the enemy meant to destroy.

## Joy Returning

Joy had been stolen from me for so long that, when it returned, it almost felt foreign. But my wife brought it back effortlessly. She carried an aura that lit up every room and a laughter that reminded me of who I had once been before the storm. From the first moment I met her, I started laughing again.

Even the ordinary moments with her felt extraordinary. I can't remember exactly what her first meal was, but I remember how it made me feel. It wasn't perfect in flavor or presentation, but it was perfect in love. I ate not just food, but care, tenderness, and the unmistakable joy of being served by someone who truly loved me.

Then there was her prayer life. My wife is a woman who knows how to intercede. I've seen her drop everything to cry out before God, sometimes pacing, sometimes kneeling, sometimes with tears streaming down her face as her words shook heaven. Whenever she prays, I am moved. It's as though I can feel the spiritual atmosphere shifting.

I learned quickly to give her the space she needs in those moments. Supporting her prayer life became one of my greatest privileges, because it reminded me that God had given me not just a partner, but a warrior.

Her beauty is undeniable—statuesque, pulchritudinous—but it is her character that shines brighter than anything outward. She embodies the qualities of a Proverbs 31 woman: wise, nurturing, strong, and God-fearing. She loves me enough to tell me when I'm wrong, to call me higher, and to remind me of the potential God has placed in me. To perform beneath that potential would not sit quietly with her—she would address it, but always in love.

Through her love, her laughter, and her truth, I finally understood the mystery of Genesis 2:24: *"And they shall be one flesh."* With her, two truly had become one.

## Freedom in Every Area of Life

For years, I lived with the shadow of Zuleika looming over my every step. Court cases, false accusations, and manipulations hung like chains around my neck. But once I was married to my wife, those chains snapped.

Zuleika became nothing more than a relic of the past. Ancient history. Even if she tried to stir trouble, it didn't matter anymore. My wife stood firmly beside me. Her love, loyalty, and faith created a fortress around us that no outside attack could penetrate.

Freedom came in every dimension of my life:

- **Spiritually**: I no longer prayed in desperation but in gratitude.
- **Emotionally**: I could breathe deeply without the weight pressing against my chest.
- **Socially**: I laughed with friends again, without fear of betrayal.
- **Financially**: I made wise, steady decisions without someone sabotaging behind the scenes.

I was not just surviving. I was finally living.

## The Love Story Fulfilled

Our story is not just about escape from the past—it's about stepping into the fullness of God's promise.

She cooked. She prayed. She loved me deeply. And in those simple acts, I saw God's redemption unfold.

When she intercedes, I feel heaven bend low. When she laughs, it feels like fresh air after being trapped in a smoke-filled room. When she speaks truth into my life, I don't feel condemned—I feel strengthened. She has the rare gift of seeing both my flaws and my potential, and of using both to push me closer to God's purpose.

She is the fulfillment of Proverbs 31. *"Favor is deceitful, and beauty is vain: but a woman that feareth the Lord, she shall be praised."*

Through her, God showed me that the ashes of the past were not the final chapter. Joy, partnership, and true love were still possible.

## Beauty for Ashes

Looking back now, I understand the wisdom of God's timing. If restoration had come too early, I would not have recognized it. If it had come on my terms, I might have mishandled it. God allowed me to walk through the fire so that when the beauty came, I knew without question it was His doing—not mine.

The ashes were real. They weren't just memories; they were pieces of me that had been burned. Ashes of betrayal that left me questioning my worth. Ashes of nights behind bars when I wondered if God still saw me. Ashes of courtroom humiliation where my name was dragged through the mud. Ashes of dreams buried before they could ever bloom.

For a long time, I thought those ashes were all I would ever have. But Isaiah 61:3 became my reality: *"To appoint unto them that mourn in Zion, to give unto them beauty for ashes, the oil of joy for mourning, the garment of praise for the spirit of heaviness."*

The "beauty" God gave wasn't just external restoration—it was deep, soul-level healing.

- **He gave me peace** where anxiety had lived. I woke up without that knot in my stomach that once greeted me every morning.
- **He gave me laughter** after years of silence. My wife's presence filled my life with a lightness I thought was gone forever.

- **He gave me partnership** where there had been betrayal. With her, I learned that true love is patient, kind, honest, and enduring.
- **He gave me purpose** where despair had threatened to take root. My scars became testimonies, my story became ministry, and my pain became a platform for God's glory.

Even the scars themselves became part of the beauty. They remind me of where I've been, but they also declare how far God has brought me. I can tell my story without shaking, without anger, without bitterness—only with gratitude.

The oil of joy replaced mourning. Where once I cried myself to sleep, now I fall asleep to whispered prayers with my wife by my side. The garment of praise replaced the spirit of heaviness. Where once I sat in silence with my head hung low, now I lift my hands freely in worship.

God did not erase my past—He redeemed it. Every tear I shed, every prayer I prayed, every humiliation I endured became part of the soil where He planted new life. And now, that new life has blossomed into beauty I could not have imagined.

What was once a valley of weeping has become a well of refreshing. What the enemy meant for evil, God truly meant for good.

## A Word to My Younger Self

If I could speak to the man I once was—the one walking into courtrooms with trembling hands, the one lying awake at night wondering if he would ever see freedom—I would say:

*"Weeping may endure for a night, but joy comes in the morning. Though the darkness feels endless now, it is not your final destination. Do not give up. Hold fast, even when the weight of despair threatens to crush you. There is a light waiting at the end*

*of this tunnel—faint, yes, but real—and it will grow brighter with each step you take.*

*God is quietly weaving something beautiful out of this chaos, stitching hope into your brokenness. Trust Him in the waiting, for from the ashes of this pain, beauty will rise. Your scars will become the proof of your strength, and your story will be a testament to resilience."*

Today, I stand free. Healed. Loved. Whole. Not because of my strength, but because of God's faithfulness.

The chains are broken. The lies are silenced. The wounds are healed. The mourning has turned to laughter.

This is the triumph of grace: that ashes do not define us, scars do not destroy us, and brokenness does not have the last word. God does.

And His final word over my life is this: *Beauty.*

# Epilogue – Walking in the Light of Restoration

"They that sow in tears shall reap in joy. He that goeth forth and weepeth, bearing precious seed, shall doubtless come again with rejoicing, bringing his sheaves with him."

— Psalm 126:5–6

## From Fire to Freedom

If I were standing before you today, sharing my story face to face, I would begin here: I walked through the fire, but it did not consume me. I lived in my own Gehenna—surrounded by accusations, betrayal, courtrooms, and sleepless nights—but I am here as living proof that the God who delivers still reigns.

There was a time when I sat in a holding cell, broken and humiliated, wondering if I would ever see freedom again. Today, I sit across the table from my wife, laughing as she sets down a meal she prepared with love. The contrast is staggering—yet it is the evidence of God's hand turning ashes into beauty.

## God's Faithfulness in My Journey

Looking back, I see clearly what I could not see then: every painful step was ordered by the Lord. He was with me when I cried through the night. He was with me when judges delayed decisions. He was with me when friends misunderstood and walked away.

Isaiah 40:31 became my anchor:

*"But they that wait upon the LORD shall renew their strength; they shall mount up with wings as eagles; they shall run, and not be weary; and they shall walk, and not faint."*

Waiting wasn't passive—it was active trust. And in that waiting, He renewed me.

## Redemption and Restoration

Romans 8:28 tells us:

*"And we know that all things work together for good to them that love God, to them who are the called according to his purpose."*

I lived this verse. The enemy meant it all for harm, but God used every accusation, every delay, every tear to shape me into the man I am today.

The greatest sign of His redemption was not just the dismissal of court cases—it was the gift of a godly wife. She embodies Proverbs 31:30:

*"Favor is deceitful, and beauty is vain: but a woman that feareth the LORD, she shall be praised."*

She is beautiful, not only outwardly but in character, in strength, and in prayer. She never judged me for what I endured. She never used my past as a weapon against me. Instead, she prays, she intercedes, she laughs with me, she challenges me, and she walks beside me as one with me. For the first time in my life, I can say: "Two have truly become one."

## Joy Restored

When I met her, I started laughing again. The joy that had been stripped from me by false accusations and years of turmoil returned in full measure. I find joy in the little things—her cooking (even when the first meal wasn't perfect, the love made it a feast), her prayers, her gentle corrections, her unwavering support.

Through her, I've learned that restoration is not abstract—it is tangible. It's in the sound of laughter returning to my home. It's in the peace of laying my head down at night without fear. It's in the beauty of shared prayers rising like incense before the Lord.

## A Testimony for Others

To the younger me—and to anyone walking through their own fire—I say this: *"Weeping may endure for a night, but joy comes in the morning"* (Psalm 30:5).

Don't give up. The tunnel may seem endless, but there is light at the end. And that light is Christ Himself. If He could bring me out, vindicate me, heal me, and give me beauty for ashes, He can and will do the same for you.

## Living in the Light

This is my testimony: I lived in Gehenna, but I now walk in freedom. The fire did not destroy me—it refined me.

- My scars remain, but they no longer bleed; they testify.
- My past is real, but it no longer defines me.
- My story began in ashes, but it ends in beauty.

And now, I live daily in the joy of restoration: loving and being loved, mentoring others, worshiping without fear, and testifying of God's goodness.

Psalm 126:5–6 is no longer just a verse to me—it is my life's song:

*"They that sow in tears shall reap in joy. He that goeth forth and weepeth, bearing precious seed, shall doubtless come again with rejoicing, bringing his sheaves with him."*

## Final Blessing

May the same God who carried me through the fire carry you.

May your ashes become beauty.

May your nights of weeping turn into mornings of joy.

May your scars become testimonies.

And may you walk boldly in the light of restoration.

## Closing Prayer

"Lord, I thank You for turning my mourning into dancing, my despair into joy, and my ashes into beauty. May this testimony encourage others to endure, to trust, and to believe that You are faithful. Let every reader who carries pain find hope in You, and may their story, like mine, be rewritten by Your redeeming hand. In Jesus' name, Amen."

# Appendix

## 1. Scripture Promises for Survivors

A collection of key Scriptures to encourage, comfort, and guide those who have faced injustice, heartbreak, or betrayal:

- **Psalm 34:18** – "The LORD is nigh unto them that are of a broken heart; and saveth such as be of a contrite spirit."
- **Isaiah 61:3** – "To grant to them that mourn in Zion… the garment of praise for the spirit of heaviness…"
- **Romans 8:28** – "And we know that all things work together for good to them that love God, to them who are called according to his purpose."
- **Lamentations 2:19** – "Pour out thy heart like water before the LORD."
- **Psalm 126:5–6** – "They that sow in tears shall reap in joy. He that goeth forth and weepeth, bearing precious seed, shall doubtless come again with rejoicing, bringing his sheaves with him."
- **Philippians 4:13** – "I can do all things through Christ which strengtheneth me."
- **Genesis 16:13** – "Thou art the God that seest me."
- **Hebrews 4:15** – "For we have not a high priest which cannot be touched with the feeling of our infirmities…"
- **Psalm 55:22** – "Cast thy burden upon the LORD, and he shall sustain thee: he shall never suffer the righteous to be moved."
- **Isaiah 43:18–19** – "Remember ye not the former things, neither consider the things of old. Behold, I will do a new thing; now it shall spring forth; shall ye not know it?"
- **Proverbs 3:5–6** – "Trust in the LORD with all thine heart; and lean not unto thine own understanding. In all thy ways acknowledge him, and he shall direct thy paths."

## Reflection Prompts

1. Which of these Scriptures speaks most to your current season of life? Why?
2. Write out the verse by hand and personalize it with your name.
3. Where in your story have you already seen God fulfill one of these promises?
4. Which promise feels hardest to believe right now? Ask God to help you trust it.

## Journal Exercise

Choose one Scripture from each theme (Comfort, Strength, Restoration). Write a short prayer around each.

# 2. Prayer and Healing Resources

## Prayer Tips

- Journal prayers daily, including lament, gratitude, and petitions.
- Write down specific fears or regrets and hand them over to God in prayer.
- Pray for those who have hurt you, seeking God's redemption for their lives as well.

## Worship as Healing

Music can carry your grief, release your heart, and reinforce God's presence.

**Lament and Expression of Grief:**

- Even If – MercyMe
- It Is Well with My Soul – Horatio Spafford
- I Surrender All – Judson W. Van DeVenter
- Precious Lord, Take My Hand – Thomas A. Dorsey
- Psalm 42 (As the Deer) – Marty Haugen
- Come to Me – Bethel Music
- You Are God Alone – Phillips, Craig & Dean

**Trust and Strength in God:**

- Oceans (Where Feet May Fail) – Hillsong United
- Way Maker – Sinach / Leeland
- Great Is Thy Faithfulness – Thomas Chisholm
- Cornerstone – Hillsong Worship
- Trust in You – Lauren Daigle
- Do It Again – Elevation Worship
- Forever – Kari Jobe

**Praise and Declaration of Victory:**

- Raise a Hallelujah – Bethel Music
- Yes I Will – Vertical Worship
- Blessed Be Your Name – Matt Redman
- Victory Is Yours – Darlene Zschech
- Shout to the Lord – Darlene Zschech
- Every Praise – Hezekiah Walker

**Restoration and Redemption:**

- Bless the Broken Road – Selah
- I Won't Give Up – Jason Mraz
- Chain Breaker – Zach Williams
- God of Miracles – Chris McClarney
- You Say – Lauren Daigle
- Redeemed – Big Daddy Weave
- Your Grace Is Enough – Matt Maher

**Tips for Using Worship Music:**

1. Play songs during devotion, prayer, or meditation.
2. Sing aloud as a spiritual release and declaration of faith.
3. Create playlists by purpose: lament, trust, victory, restoration.
4. Repeat songs during milestones to reinforce hope and healing.

## Reflection Prompts

1. When was the last time you prayed with complete honesty—without censoring anger, sadness, or confusion?
2. What burdens are you holding onto that you could write down and surrender in prayer?
3. Who in your life needs your prayers for redemption—even if they hurt you?

## Journal Exercise

Write a letter to God as if you were speaking to a close friend. Pour out your raw feelings, then end with: *"Lord, I place this in Your hands."*

# 3. A Note to Pastors, Counselors, and Churches

This book is written to encourage those who have suffered injustice, heartbreak, and betrayal. Pastors, counselors, and ministry leaders can use it to:

- Teach lament as a spiritual discipline leading to healing and hope.
- Guide individuals in rebuilding trust, relationships, and identity.

- Use Scripture to anchor hope and restoration in difficult circumstances.
- Demonstrate how God's faithfulness transforms trials into testimony.
- Encourage survivors to engage in prayer, worship, and community for emotional and spiritual restoration.

## Key Considerations for Ministry Leaders

- Listen patiently and validate the survivor's experience.
- Encourage journaling, Scripture study, and worship as tools for processing pain.
- Emphasize God's timing and sovereignty in all areas of restoration.
- Avoid minimizing grief or forcing forgiveness; allow the process to be personal and Spirit-led.

## Reflection Prompts

1. How has the church (or spiritual leaders) responded to your pain in the past—helpfully or unhelpfully?
2. What do you wish leaders understood about your experience?
3. How could you, in time, use your story to help the church minister to others?

## Journal Exercise

Write out your ideal response: If a pastor or counselor asked, *"How can we walk with you?"* what would you want to say?

# 4. Encouragement to the Reader

If you are reading this, know this: **God sees you.** He knows your pain. He is already at work behind the scenes, preparing a path of restoration—even if you cannot see it yet.

## Five Anchors to Hold Onto

1. **Lament is powerful** – Pour out your grief, anger, and sorrow before the Lord. It is worship and healing, not weakness.
2. **Faithful endurance pays off** – Even when life seems unjust, trust God's timing and presence.
3. **Forgiveness sets you free** – It does not excuse wrongs but releases your heart into peace.
4. **God's orchestration is perfect** – What the enemy intends for harm, God can use for ultimate good.
5. **Restoration is multidimensional** – Spiritually, emotionally, socially, and relationally, God rebuilds what was lost when you surrender to Him.

## Jeremiah 29:11:

"For I know the thoughts that I think toward you, saith the LORD, thoughts of peace, and not of evil, to give you an expected end."

## Reflection Prompts

1. What "ashes" in your life is God calling you to hand over for transformation?
2. Where have you already seen small "streams in the desert" (Isaiah 43:19) in your journey?
3. If you could tell your younger self one thing, what would it be?

## Journal Exercise

Write a short testimony paragraph as if you were speaking to someone who is where you once were. End it with a Scripture of hope.

# Closing Prayer

"Lord, I thank You for every lesson, every trial, and every moment of Your presence that carried me through. May this story encourage others to trust You, even when life seems unjust. May those reading find hope, courage, and restoration in Your hands. Lord, let their hearts be open to Your redemption, their lives be renewed, and their paths be guided by Your wisdom and love. In Jesus' name, Amen."

**Back Cover**

*Living in Gehenna: Faith in the Midst of Fire* tells the gripping true story of Cordell Brown, a man who entered marriage full of hope—only to find himself trapped in a furnace of emotional torment, false accusations, and spiritual warfare.

Behind the smiles and promises lurked control, betrayal, and hidden pain. What should have been a covenant of love became a crucible of lies and manipulation. Yet this is not a story of defeat—it is a testimony of endurance, divine intervention, and the unshakable presence of God.

Through sleepless nights, courtroom battles, and relentless attacks, Cordell discovered that no furnace is too hot and no trial too dark when God walks beside you. Rooted in Scripture and illuminated by faith, his journey offers courage, wisdom, and hope for anyone facing betrayal, injustice, or deep personal trials.

This book will remind you:

- That God sees your pain.
- That His Word sustains you in the fire.
- That He can turn ashes into beauty, and mourning into joy.

*Living in Gehenna* is more than a memoir—it is a survival manual for the soul, a witness to God's faithfulness, and a call to trust Him in the very midst of the fire.